The Smooth Embrace

Chapter One

"If you don't mind let me know you're clowning!" Whitney Russell paced the floor of the comfortable B and B and attempted her best to keep her voice quiet. Her week had begun off awful and was deteriorating by the moment.

"Simone, I need to stay at your B and B. I drove the distance to town from Sulphur, and I anticipate arriving for no less than two or three days."

The more seasoned lady with a head loaded with silver hair took a gander at Whitney through contrite eyes. "I comprehend, sweetie, yet there is nothing I can do. A voyaging bike club landed in Lake Charles yesterday and saved every one of the ten of my rooms."

Whitney crushed the extension of her nose to attempt and balance her developing cerebral pain. "Don't you have two crisis save rooms in the cellar? It is safe to say that they are accessible?"

"Normally they would be, however the whole storm cellar is getting revamped so it isn't reasonable right at this point. I would instruct you to call Al to check whether you could stay in one of the extra rooms over his eatery, however he as of now called to let me know he'd taken in a couple away guests."

"So essentially, I'm out of choices." Whitney couldn't trust her good fortune. She'd carried on with her whole life in Lake Charles, Louisiana, except for leaving to school, and had just as of late moved to Sulphur in the wake of getting her fantasy work. Presently, in addition to the fact that she was back around the local area after just months of being without end, yet she likewise had no spot to sit tight.

"I figure I could call Theresa." Theresa had been her companion since they were in kindergarten.

"Do regardless you converse with Theresa?" Simone inquired.

"Obviously I do. I've just been living in Sulphur for six months so I haven't been gone that long."

"At the Christmas party, Theresa declared that she was gone to Europe for a year. She simply left two or three weeks back."

"It's hard to believe, but it's true," Whitney said, snapping her fingers. "I disregarded that." Whitney hadn't been back for Christmas such as she'd guaranteed, yet Theresa had called her to educate her concerning her temporary position at a prestigious workmanship firm in Paris. She hadn't got notification from Stef since she landed in Paris however gave careful consideration to call her when she got herself out of this chaos.

"There is one other choice," Simone said with a slippery grin.

"I don't care for that look, Simone. What are you considering?"

"All things considered, I just so happen to know a young fellow who is back around the local area and has a pleasant ample trailer in his terrace. Consideration to take a think about who that individual is?"

Whitney didn't have to think about who Simone was alluding to. She definitely knew. Regardless of the possibility that she hadn't known, she would've possessed the capacity to figure just by the guileful look present all over.

"Give me a chance to figure. You're alluding to your nephew."

"I beyond any doubt am," Simone addressed catching her hands together. "He's staying in the old Wheeler home, and incidentally he's leasing the trailer in his back yard. I'm certain he'd be cheerful to see you."

I profoundly question that. "He's perpetually discontent to see anybody, particularly me."

"Gracious sweetie, that is not genuine. Both of you were as chummy growing up."

That might have been genuine, yet that was quite a while back. "All things considered, things change, however now that I'm really back around the local area, I figure I should quit delaying the unavoidable and head over to his place."

"Great! We couldn't have you out in the roads with no spot to rest. You and my nephew are more than welcome to return a couple of hours for supper. I heard they have great nourishment in Sulphur, however nothing beats my cooking. Let me simply snatch a scratch pad to scribble down his location for you in the event that you've overlooked it."

After Simone left the room, Whitney sank down into a close-by sofa. What a madly insane week. When she'd found the occupation as the Online networking Operations Supervisor at Custom-made Modernity, she could scarcely contain her energy. The attire and underwear online membership was made by creators, Carla Jones and Brad Woods. Their new web application permitted men and ladies to finish a review that included data on their own style, size, estimations, and have a Custom-made Complexity beautician handpick their apparel, nightwear or underwear. Also, the application offered styling counsel in light of the best kind of dress for his or her body sort.

Whitney had doubtlessly in her psyche that Customized Complexity would be the following best thing to hit the garments market. In any case, the site and application dispatch was in only seven days, and they had a genuine hiccup in their arrangement. Whitney had no clue what had pushed her to persuade Carla and Brad that she had the assets to spare the official dispatch party. She wasn't certain she'd really halted to consider what she was doing before she had jumped in her auto and drove back to the place where she grew up resolved to discover an answer.

After Simone came back with a piece of paper close by, she gave the location to Whitney and gave her an empowering embrace. "It's fine, sweetie. Both of you go route back, so simply act naturally."

***

After fifteen minutes, Whitney was remaining before a somewhat worn red entryway attempting to exemplify Simone's words.

"You can do this. Simply act naturally and attempt to unwind." The energy talk did little to quiet her nerves. She adverted her eyes to the container of red paint toward the side of the patio and appreciated the snow white yard railing that had as of late been painted. It might sound insane, however she knew those paint strokes anyplace. The home looked a great deal superior to the way old man Wheeler had abandoned it.

Changing her light blue scarf and beige spring coat, she took a full breath before thumping on the front entryway. When he didn't answer, she thumped again somewhat harder than some time recently.

"So common," she murmured. It was much the same as him not to answer when somebody thumped. In the event that she had his number, she would've called first. Before she got an opportunity to mutter a couple of more decision words, the entryway swung open generally as she connected her arm to thump a third time.

She wasn't certain in the event that it was the energy of the entryway swinging open while her hand was in midair or the stun of her eyes arrival on the limited she thought she'd most likely never see again that made her bumble. Her feet appeared to have their very own psyche as she stumbled over the yard tangle and tumbled forward, not able to adjust herself.

As she felt herself free-falling into the hall of the home, solid strong arms firmly grasped her around her waist and flipped her around.

All the air hurried out of her lungs at the speed of his moves. It was sufficiently hard to appreciate him from a separation and not salivate, not to mention face him with his profound hazel eyes peering into her chestnut cocoa ones as though getting her from an awful fall was simply some portion of his ordinary obligations.

He hadn't talked yet, and the way that he wasn't talking was making her to a great degree apprehensive. This was the man she'd regularly pondered when she played those diversions with sweethearts that made you answer a huge amount of uncomfortable inquiries. Questions about your first kiss, first love, the special case that will always be a nagging memory or the one that made you extremely upset. Each and every time she needed to answer an inquiry regarding adoration, energy, and sorrow, there was one and only name that left her lips-one name that dependably attacked her contemplations.

"Chad Harris," she whispered, conveying considerably more musings to the front line of her psyche. One of his brilliant chestnut tattooed arms connected with brush a couple strands of her wavy Harris hair from her face, while the other kept up its tight grasp around her body.

"Whitney Russell. What exactly do I owe the joy?"

His voice was profound. More enchanting than she recalled. She opened her mouth to talk, however no words turned out. What is this disastrous situation?

Chapter Two

Chad looked into the eyes of the lady who was never too a long way from his musings. She was considerably more delightful in individual than she was in his fantasies. Whitney... He'd been readied to advise whomever was at his way to take a climb since he was path behind on his work. At that point he'd opened the entryway and saw her. He hadn't seen her in years, and truly, couldn't trust despite everything she appeared to be identical. Scratch that. She looked far better than the last time they'd run into each other.

Two or three her components hadn't changed. Three light cocoa spots were still on her right sanctuary. He adored the rich state of her lips lips that, at one point before, had him so spellbound, he regularly got himself staring off into space about them. In any case, a ton had changed as well. Her hair was longer than he recalled, and there was a light redden on her cheeks that was either the aftereffect of a little cosmetics or of him holding her so close. Her cappuccino composition was brighter, smoother. As usual, his body immediately reacted to hers. His fingers were yearning to investigate her, however he controlled the inclination.

He helped her stand to her feet that were encased in short dull chestnut boots and saw that her body shape was distinctive. Indeed, even in her jacket, he could tell there were bends there that she never had. Gone was the body of an adolescent or a youthful grown-up. She was currently a twenty-six year old lady, and despite the fact that there was still a blamelessness about her, he could tell she was not the same young lady he once knew. He would have kept on respecting her peacefully, yet he understood she hadn't addressed his inquiry.

"Thus, what's going on with you?" he solicited rather from rehashing his first question.

"Indeed, I've been fine following the last time we talked, and you made me extremely upset in two. A couple tears here and there yet that was years back. How are you?"

He shook his head with a constrained giggle. Still the same Whitney. Despite the fact that she was sweet, she was additionally a legitimate sharp shooter. She generally called him on his poo. That was another reason he had fallen so hard for her when they were more youthful.

"In the event that I review, I wasn't the special case who broke a heart that day. It appeared to be really clear four years back that you had a decision to make, and I wasn't the right one."

"Since you got me into a tough situation when, in fact, your brain had as of now been made up before we'd had that discussion."

"Also, I would have readily moved mountains to make you glad in the event that you would have given me any sign that you needed our relationship to proceed."

"We never stood a chance, right Chad ?" She folded her arms over her mid-section. "Your words, not mine. You would have moved mountains for me on the off chance that I had given you a sign, regardless of the way that I gave you a few? Is it true that you are certain consummation our relationship had nothing to do with you being terrified?"

He murmured as he stuffed his hands in the pockets of his pants. He didn't said those definite words, yet it seemed like something he would've said. How frequently had he got his phone to call her and perceive how she was doing? How often had he thought about whether the choice to end their relationship wasn't shared yet rather more his decision or hers? Chad was an extremely private individual, however at one time, he'd told Whitney insider facts he thought he'd never impart to anybody-mysteries that made him helpless and feel more human than he'd ever felt some time recently. To a few, they didn't comprehend why feeling human was an awful thing. Be that as it may, jumping into the internal workings of a PC system framework required fixation and core interest. Two things he appeared to need when he let sentiments or feelings cloud his psyche. He was certain a few techies could permit themselves to both be powerless and be incredible at their occupation, however he wasn't your normal tech nerd. He frequently concealed his ability, and when individuals saw an athletic person with the tattoos on his arms, they had no clue that he was one of the best web engineers in the Midwest. He didn't fit the run of the mill profile.

"That is not how I recall that it."

"Some way or another, that doesn't shock me." She was irritated, and he wasn't improving it any.

"Things being what they are, is that what you made a trip for? To let me know what a savage I was to you a couple of years prior."

"I never called you any names and that is not why I'm here." She looked uncomfortable, and surprisingly since she'd faltered into his home, he perceived how restless she was.

"What is it Whitney? Is everything OK?" he asked abruptly anxious that something was genuinely off-base.

"No, everything isn't alright. I require your assistance. I found a vocation as an Online networking Operations Administrator for a new business, and with just days until we dispatch our web application, we discovered that the organization that was planning our site and application just went gut up. I was a piece of the procuring process for this organization, so I feel somewhat mindful. We're stuck a noteworthy spot, and I was trusting you could bail me out."

He investigated her arguing eyes and knew he couldn't advise her no. Despite the fact that she was correct, it was a to a great degree occupied time for him. In the wake of leaving his occupation in the FBI digital security division eight months back, he'd begun doing autonomous web engineer work simply like he'd done in school. He had more than twenty customers, and the month of April was normally spent guaranteeing that everything was up to code on his customer's sites. He'd been doing random web engineer work since he was sixteen, and spring was dependably the busiest time.

"What's the organization?"

"Custom-made Modernity. One of the proprietors, Carla Jones, proprietor of Exposed Refinement undergarments boutique in Sulphur, collaborated with her life partner and co-proprietor, Brad Woods, the maker and originator of University Life and T.R. Night."

"I've certainly known about Brad Woods. I adore his apparel line. I heard a few people here in Lake Charles discuss his engagement to Carla this past December."

"I'm not shocked. News of their engagement got a great deal of media consideration in the Midwest states. That is the reason Customized Complexity must be extraordinary."

"Things being what they are, how soon would they require the web application and site assembled?"

"Five days, the dispatch gathering is in seven."

"Poop, that is soon. It's fortunate I work quick."

"Does that mean you'll offer me out?" He some assistance with missing seeing the twinkle in her eye at whatever point she got amped up for something. He'd known he would offer her before he some assistance with evening realized what she required help with. Just before he opened his mouth to concur, he got a quick look at a white envelope on the table in his lobby. What preferable individual to help me over Whitney?

"I'll bail you out under one condition?"

She squinted her eyes in distrust. "What's the condition?"

"I'll complete your site and application in two days, and your group can test everything out, except you need to spend the other two days offering me some assistance with preparing for my honors service that I additionally need you to go to with me."

"Honor for what?"

"Work I did when I was with the FBI. My previous director says I have to take a shot at my relationship building abilities."

"You don't say," she said. "At that point I additionally have a solicitation to add to that. I don't have a spot to sit tight. Your close relative's place is reserved as is Al's."

"You can stay in the trailer out back. I simply put it on Airbnb, so it's prepared to go. Does that mean you acknowledge my offer?"

She scrunched her nose before reacting. "I'm not certain if Carla and Brad will consent to me staying in Lake Charles for five days."

"At that point you ought to inquire. The grants service is in Sulphur, so it works out." He folded his arms over his mid-section as she took out her phone to call her managers. Chad may not be a social butterfly, but rather he comprehended edginess, and there was undoubtedly in his brain that an organization on the very edge of a gigantic site uncover would remain absolutely determined to guarantee the dispatch was fruitful.

Chapter Three

"Whitney, that is awesome to listen. Kindly tell Chad that we truly value all the work he did."

"I will," Whitney said to Carla's sister, Summer Jones, who was in Sulphur for the dispatch. "He was resolved to complete it in two days, and I once in a while saw him while he was taking a shot at everything."

"All things considered, it is completely phenomenal! We as a whole cherish it. It looks superior to the fake site we saw from the organization we were working with some time recently. We have our test bunch looking at everything now, except I'm certain the dispatch will be immaculate."

With Carla and Brad owning their own organizations, visiting for their attire lines, beginning another business, and arranging a wedding, Summer had ventured into help with Customized Advancement. Despite the fact that Whitney had dependably been near her cousin Josie growing up, she was a just kid, and she appreciated the fellowship between the Jones kin.

"You know, Chad has an extraordinary individual site, yet I couldn't locate a nice picture of him anyplace."

Whitney grinned. She'd met Summer at the engagement party for Carla and Brad a couple of months back. They'd gotten along promptly, and every so often, visited on the telephone.

"He abhors taking pictures," she said with a chuckle. "Indeed, he detests online networking when all is said in done. We've clearly never seen eye to eye on that."

"That clarifies why he needs your assistance planning for that grants service. Unless, there's a whole other world to your relationship than only a person you grew up with like you guaranteed."

Whitney made a sound as if to speak. "The narrative of Chad and I is similar to an arduous sitcom. Great before all else yet disillusioning at last."

"Ok, so there is history. One day, I trust you feel slanted to share this story."

"Better believe it, possibly one day I will."

They talked somewhat more before Whitney finished the call. As she sat on the main rich seat in the trailer, she contemplated how diverse Chad was from the last time she saw him. Amid that time, he was twenty-three and had recently been enrolled by the FBI. From various perspectives, he had still been a kid attempting to take care of business. Presently, at twenty-seven, he'd certainly developed, and despite the fact that the FBI had a ton to do with it, Whitney expected that the demise of his dad a year ago had something to do with it also.

After she'd questioned Chad on everything required for the Customized Modernity site and application, she'd allowed him to sit unbothered to work. As guaranteed, he'd taken care of business in two days, however now, it was the ideal opportunity for section two of the assentation.

Whitney thumped on his secondary passage. They should meet for their first session this evening, and she had chosen to warmly call their sessions Acculturating Chad 101. He loathed the name, which obviously, made her adoration it much more.

When he didn't answer to her second thump, she let herself in. She got out his name two or three times and didn't get a reaction. At last, she spotted him lying on the love seat resting.

He looked so tranquil when he dozed. He didn't wheeze. Scarcely moved. One solid arm laid to his side while the other was hung over his eyes. He wore his standard clothing - a white tee and Levis - and was shoeless with one lower leg traversed the other.

"Magnificence and the monster," she whispered. When they initially began dating the mid year after her sophomore year of secondary school, he frequently alluded to them as the magnificence and the mammoth. Not just was it her most loved film growing up, however Chad had been the primary individual to ever call her delightful and really made her vibe the words he'd talked.

She tenderly sat in favor of the love seat next to him. She truly shouldn't be this nearby, yet she couldn't help herself. It had been years since she could respect his solid manly elements as he rested. While most young men had been petitioning God for facial hair, Chad had worn a flawlessly trimmed whiskers that made every one of the young ladies of Lake Charles swoon over him. He had it all - insight, desire, devastatingly nice looking components, and wonderful eyes that appeared to look into your spirit. Goodness, I miss him. Missing Chad despite the fact that she hadn't seen him in years was intense. Seeing him these past couple days, regardless of how short, would most likely make her miss him considerably more when she came back to Sulphur.

He evacuated the arm covering his eyes pretty much as she was going to hold up. "I see regardless you wear that jasmine and vanilla oil mix." His voice was imposing and grateful. "You recognize what that scent dependably did to me."

She looked down at his arm that had wound around her waist sticking her to the sofa. When he inclined toward the elbow of his other arm, it united their countenances. She'd lost check of how long she'd spent imagining about his face.

"I thumped on the indirect access, yet figured you wouldn't see any problems on the off chance that I let myself in."

"My pleasure in my home whenever."

Her eyes dropped to his lips before she could stop herself. His psyche might have interested her over the span of their six year relationship, however it was his looks that had frequently abandoned her puzzled. His lips twisted to the side in a grin, making her turn away her look back to his eyes. Generally, he was still the same Chad she recalled. He'd generally been immaculate male, yet now, he was more manly and overflowed a hotness that appeared to be significantly more hazardous. She likewise saw a trouble in his eyes that hadn't been there some time recently.

"It made me extremely upset when I found out about your father. I'm so sad for your misfortune."

He quickly turned away as though he needed to say something. "What is it?" she inquired.

"Simply something I've been pondering." He moved on the love seat. "In spite of the fact that I regarded my father's wish not to have a burial service, I thought you would have in any event ceased by the dedication my auntie had at her B and B."

She moaned before reacting. "I stopped by."

"I didn't see you."

I needed it that way. Nobody aside from Theresa had known she'd been around the local area that day, and she'd always remember how harmed she felt when she'd looked at Chad. "I got around the local area the morning of your father's commemoration. You hadn't formally moved to Lake Charles yet. When I touched base at Simone's B and B, I got a quick look at you in the lawn sitting by the lake, so I advised Stef to head inside, and I went to you to give you the same bolster you gave me when my mother had passed away. I was sufficiently close to touch your shoulder when I caught you talking."

Chad squinted his eyes in disarray. "Who was I conversing with?"

"I didn't see any other person there, so I expect you were conversing with yourself." She looked down at her hands as she squirmed with the base of her shirt. "You were discussing us, saying we would have been exceptional off as companions and not mates."

There was more to what he had said, however Whitney quit talking when she saw acknowledgment set in his eyes. "Whitney, after my dad was determined to have stage four prostate tumor, he began to blur quick, and since we knew our discussions were restricted, he let me know that he needed me to begin discussing him as though he were at that point gone."

"Sounds like your father," she said with a slight grin. "So you were conversing with him at the lake?"

"Yes, I was. That was the main discussion I'd had with him really being gone, however." His eyes held hers. "When you caught me discussing how we ought to have remained companions, it's not what you think. When we initially began dating, you were blameless and sweet, while I was the finished inverse. I might have been brilliant, yet I was careless and had nothing to offer you."

She shook her head in difference. "We met as children, and however you lived hours away, we made it work long separation all through secondary school and school. I didn't anticipate that you will be anybody other than yourself."

"That is not all you anticipated."

Whitney looked away, not able to look at him without flinching. She knew where their discussion was going next, and she wasn't prepared to examine that. "Indeed, I figure we both committed errors, yet I didn't stop over to go over our past. I halted by with the goal that we can chip away at your relationship building abilities before your grants service. Do you think we can put the past behind us... for the present?"

She couldn't tell on the off chance that he was diminished or disillusioned by her recommendation. Likely, a tad bit of both. "Yes, that is fine." He found her napping when he pulled her down to him. "I'm happy you're here to offer assistance."

She settled her head in the law breaker of his neck, realizing that the embrace was more about the implicit words that waited in the room, instead of her helping him, yet she relished the grasp. "I as of now owe you an a debt of gratitude is in order for sparing the Custom-made Advancement dispatch." She turned her head with the goal that she was near his ear. "What's more, I'm happy I'm here as well."

Chapter Four

Thirty hours, twelve minutes, and thirty-seven seconds. That is to what extent Chad had been doing whatever it takes not to kiss Whitney. The initial forty-eight hours she had been around the local area didn't tally since he was buckling down on the site and application. He didn't begin desiring her taste until yesterday evening when he'd woken up to her on the lounge chair. Notwithstanding when he was resting, he contemplated kissing her.

When they separated four years prior, he wasn't simply losing the individual he thought he would spend whatever is left of his existence with, he had lost his closest companion. His partner. The individual that knew him superior to anything anybody.

"Chad, you need to quit squirming," Whitney said as they strolled from the parking garage to the eatery. "You've referred to Josie for whatever length of time that you've known me, and he let me know you've as of now met Rick as well."

"I'm not squirming," he said, knowing he was telling a falsehood. Josie was Whitney's cousin and a decent companion of his. He'd met Josie's life partner Rick once, and he loved her too. Be that as it may, this evening he needed to put into practice what Whitney and him had been taking a shot at, and whatever he could consider was the manner by which her kisses dependably quieted him not at all like whatever else.

"Truly, how are you going to make an acknowledgment discourse when you can't meet with Josie and Rick without breaking out into a sweat?"

He promptly quit strolling. "You believe they're going to make me give a discourse?"

She flashed him a thoughtful grin. "You might be the most brilliant person I know, however you can be so negligent some of the time. I feel that is presumably what your boss was attempting to indicate when he instructed you to take a shot at your social aptitudes."

Before she even completed her sentence, he knew she was correct. "Why is Josie going by Lake Charles once more?"

"Since my father and his guardians moved to Monroe, and we both live in Sulphur now, he said he needed to convey Rick here to see where he grew up in light of the fact that we don't know when we'll be back to visit."

Her notice of Sulphur was an update that he was on re-appropriated time with Whitney. To be completely forthright, it felt like their whole relationship had been on re-appropriated time.

"Try not to go there now," she said interfering with his musings before addressing the entertainer. He didn't need to ask her what she implied. She'd generally known him so well.

"All things considered, on the off chance that it isn't two of the most youthful extraordinary eight individuals. Somewhat late not surprisingly," Josie said.

Chad giggled as he dapped clench hands with Josie and welcomed Rick. "Man, you generally needed that name to get on. Wouldn't you be able to consider an option that is superior to the immense eight?"

"I could have, yet that would have taken totally an excess of vitality."

Josie was additionally an individual from the considerable eight and had made the name when they had all been working at the lake in Lake Charles more than one summer break. Josie and Chad's more established sibling Tyler had quite recently graduated school and hadn't discovered employments yet while Josie and Whitney were beginning school in the fall.

"How's Tyler?" Josie inquired.

"He's still abroad." It had astonished him and his father when Tyler had abruptly selected in the Armed force. Chad constantly figured it had something to do with dismissal by Alana - another extraordinary eight part - however Tyler never let him know reality, and Chad never inquired.

"I halted by Simone's place before today and she let me know that Isaac was contemplating moving back to town."

"Better believe it, I conversed with him a month ago. It will be decent to have another person from the first group here since Kiera and Theresa as of late left, as well. Didn't think I'd at long last move to Lake Charles pretty much as the staying three incredible eight individuals had moved away."

"I knew the name would get on," Josie said waving a finger noticeable all around.

"I prefer not to separate this manly relationship," Whitney said with a chuckle. "Be that as it may, Chad, don't you have some homework you ought to be taking a shot at?"

He gritted his teeth and frowned at her, which just made Whitney giggle harder. His glare didn't stage her, and her chuckle was making his jeans somewhat more tightly than normal.

"What's the homework?" Rick asked despite the fact that he was almost certain Whitney had questioned her and Josie.

"I need to take a shot at my relationship building abilities, and my first task is to associate with somebody I don't have the foggiest idea about that well and be imminent with sharing data about myself."

Rick gave Josie a shrewd grin before looking back at Chad . "All things considered, thinking of you as scarcely said two words to me the first occasion when we met, this ought to be intriguing. I've effectively heard you visit more this evening than I suspected you would. In this way, Chad , let me know about yourself."

Chad moaned. Despite the fact that it was a basic inquiry, he never knew where to begin. Do I begin with my youth? My vocation? My gang childhood?

"Simply discuss what you're doing now," Whitney said, perusing his contemplations. "You don't need to share excessively. Simply enough so that the individual feels associated with you somehow."

Taking Whitney's recommendation, he made an effort not to overthink his reaction.

***

"Both of you look great together."

Whitney quit watching Chad and Josie and looked over at Rick who was remaining next to her on the walkway.

"We finished our relationship years back."

"So had your cousin and I, yet we got back together, and now, we're locked in. Tip top Occasions is notwithstanding arranging our wedding. We've ended up at ground zero from the primary day we strolled once again into each other's lives. That could happen to you and Chad ."

Rick and Josie had been cleaning specialist of honor and best man in their companion's wedding. The women of Tip top Occasions that were arranging their companion's wedding had educated them that they needed to work next to each other after not representing two years. Whitney needed to advise her that there was no chance that would happen, however she would not like to nonchalance the cheerful look in Rick's eyes.

"Despite everything we have a ton to discuss."

"At that point you need to talk it out. There's a reason you returned to Lake Charles to request Chad 's assistance, and there's a reason Chad moved to Lake Charles having never lived here."

"I get what you're stating, however our timing has dependably been off. We go to Sulphur the day after tomorrow for his grants function, and afterward he's coming back to Lake Charles."

"All things considered, you both are as one now, so there's no time like the present to hash things out. Take it from somebody who attempted to disregard her fate. At the point when destiny comes thumping, you better reply. Imagine a scenario in which are my slightest two most loved words in the lexicon.

"By what means would I be able to tell on the off chance that he's still into me as well?"

Whitney snickered when Rick's eyes built. "Nectar, I'll imagine that you didn't simply make an inquiry with such a conspicuous answer. In the event that you truly need to know whether the sparkles are still there, why not kiss him?"

***

Whitney was all the while pondering Rick's recommendation when they touched base back to Chad 's place.

"Is everything OK?" he solicited when they got out from the auto. She watched him for a few moments, debating on what to say next.

"Could I make a genuine inquiry?"

"Shoot." Not at all like the uneasiness Chad had amid supper when Rick made inquiries, Whitney saw he didn't appear to be on edge at all at this point.

"Is it accurate to say that you are upbeat? That is to say, really glad?"

His eyes became genuine as he ventured nearer to her. "I haven't been glad in quite a while," he conceded. "I used to be. Quite a while back. I even tricked myself into trusting I was presently... until you touched base on my doorstep. I miss the individual I was the point at which we were as one."

Her voice was scarcely over a whisper when she talked. "Me as well."

Chapter Five

Chad prided himself on dissecting a circumstance and knowing the following individual's turn before they made it. His scientific aptitudes had made him extraordinary at his digital security work with the FBI, so he was certain when Whitney swung to stroll back to the trailer, he wouldn't see her again that night.

The thump on his indirect access found him napping, however he knew it was her even before he opened it. When she ventured into the encased sun deck, she bit her base lip. A sign she was apprehensive. What is she supposing about? He needed to ask her, however they both stayed quiet until at long last, she talked.

"Four years prior, when I everything except requested that you accept the occupation with my father and uncle's organization, I'd been totally out of line. I've pondered that discussion we had, and I needed you to realize that I wasn't attempting to change the individual you were."

"You're father never thought I was sufficient to be with you, and I comprehended why he felt that path since you're his just youngster. What I hadn't anticipated that was for you would give me a final proposal when you had said, I couldn't be with you unless I worked for your dad."

She put her head down before meeting his eyes. "That wasn't the reason I gave you the final offer."

"At that point what was the reason?"

She bit her base lip once more. "You know I cherished your father, yet you additionally realize that your mom abandoning him, your sibling, and you for another man crushed him."

Chad recoiled at the notice of his mom. He and Tyler concurred never to discuss the lady who'd left her crew without a second look. "What did my mom leaving need to do with us?"

"Nothing at first. Be that as it may, then your father called me one day directly after I'd graduated and let me know he was around the local area going to your close relative. I met him at Simone's B and B and that is the point at which he let me know he'd conversed with my dad."

"My father experienced childhood in Lake Charles, and our fathers couldn't stand each other. That is the reason my father was so restless to move a couple of towns over. What might they be able to have conceivably examined?"

At the point when Whitney rearranged from one foot to the next, Chad had a shocking feeling that he comprehended what discussion had occurred before she even said it.

"Since your mother worked for the FBI, and the FBI had quite recently selected you, he requested that my dad offer you a vocation. In the event that you review, my father and uncle had quite recently chosen to extend the business to California. In spite of the fact that Josie and I never needed to assume control over the organization, my father called me after I met with your father and let me know he would acknowledge our relationship in the event that we both took employments working for him. I figure, after every one of those years, our fathers had at last discovered something they concurred on."

"To the detriment of their youngsters' satisfaction. The arrangement didn't work." He was irritated in spite of the fact that it felt wrong to be irate at his father who was no more here to account for himself. He saw Whitney quickly brush her ring finger before dropping both hands to the side. He quickly felt like a rascal for how he'd acted the night she'd drawn closer him about the occupation and moving to California.

"I ought to have known the final offer wasn't your thought."

"It's not your blame. I ought to have let you know about what our fathers were doing."

"Why didn't you simply come right out and let me know?"

"I was going to, however then you hauled out the wedding band that fit in with your grandma and let me know that the lady you were going to propose to that night could never compel you into a choice such as that. At that point you said that you ought to have known we never stood a chance the primary day you looked at me since you required a solid lady. A genuine lady. Somebody with more background. Not a frightened young lady who had confidence in the force of positive thinking and saw life through rose shaded glasses... "

As her voice trailed off, Chad felt a kick in his gut. He recollected distinctively all the terrible things he had said to her. Things he never envisioned saying.

"I'm sad, Whitney. I hadn't implied the things I said that night."

"In a few ways, I think you did." She delicately touched his arm. "Being around you these previous couple of days are additionally making me recollect what you experienced in your past that presumably drove you to say them."

"That night, you'd helped me to remember my mother. She was perpetually discontent with my father and had attempted unsuccessfully to change him before running off with some person who worked for the CIA. She began a whole new family and existence with him, overlooking us. In some distorted way, you giving me the final proposal and overlooking every one of the fantasies we had, uncovered a hurt from my mother's dismissal that I thought I'd covered. My father didn't converse with me for a long time once I joined the FBI, and I don't think he comprehended that I would not like to join the FBI to be similar to her. I just couldn't help the way that working for the FBI was the ideal employment for me."

"It was, and I'm happy despite everything you chose to accept the employment. You don't need to let me know that you quit when your father became ill. I know you all around ok to know you most likely felt regretful for joining the department and spending his remaining years doing something he never needed you to take in any case. I'm likewise certain my dad said more than a couple of decision words to you over the span of our relationship that prompted your disappointment that night."

She was correct. Her dad had said more than a couple of rude things to him while they were dating, yet he didn't need her rationalizing how he carried on that night. He ventured nearer to her to guarantee that she saw precisely what he said next.

"Whitney, correspondence has never been my strength and that night was the same. I was a rascal to you, and I will everlastingly be sad for how I acted. You've generally been my greatest supporter. I ought to have proposed to you like I'd arranged and comprehended that together, regardless of what occupation we had or what state we lived in, we could succeed the length of we were as one. In those days, I was still youthful from multiple points of view and frail in the matter of how a person like me could arrive a young lady like you. Be that as it may, there will never be another Whitney Russell, and I've generally known that I am so fortunate to have you in my life."

Chad brushed away two or three tears that had tumbled down her cheeks. "I've sat tight years for that expression of remorse."

"I'm sad it took so yearn for me to offer it to you." He was done being frightened and second speculating everything when it came to Whitney. Despite everything he had far to go to demonstrate the amount he gave it a second thought, yet right now, all he needed to do was kiss the lips he'd been contemplating for a considerable length of time.

She anxiously met his lips in a kiss that was loaded with so much feeling, he really wanted to draw her significantly nearer. He felt the kiss in all aspects of his body, and simply like the greater part of Whitney's past kisses, it was great.

Chapter Six

All through the whole night, Whitney watched Chad work the room. He'd effectively visited with different individuals from the FBI who were getting respected for their work alongside their families, yet despite everything he appeared to be apprehensive to give an acknowledgment discourse.

"You'll be fine," Whitney whispered into his ear. They were sitting at a dinner table encompassed by individuals from Chad's previous digital group, and she could feel his leg shaking under the table. She was so pleased with him, and despite the fact that they couldn't discharge the careful subtle elements of why he was getting regarded, she knew it was a major ordeal.

"Why the hellfire do they make you give an acknowledgment discourse when you get a recompense?" he whispered back. Whitney attempted her best to keep her snicker as peaceful as could reasonably be expected.

"That is normally what's accepted when the grant beneficiary is available. We honed your discourse all of yesterday, you'll be fine."

A couple of more minutes passed and his previous director went to the platform to say a couple words before Chad made that big appearance. He's going to pop a vein on the off chance that he doesn't extricate up. She knew of one and only approach to motivate him to quiet down. When he was called to the stage, she pulled him in for a profound kiss without minding who viewed. To most, it seemed, by all accounts, to be a salutary kiss, however Chad 's wily grin let her realize that he knew precisely why she'd kissed him so completely.

"Much thanks to you," he said before making that big appearance to acknowledge his honor for being the lead digital pro to find the programmers for a prominent money related organization. His discourse was perfect, and in the event that she hadn't known how frightened Chad Harris was of open talking, she would have never speculated by his deliverance. What she saw considerably more was the level of appreciation he got from others in participation. He'd been enrolled while he was in graduate school, and despite the fact that they hadn't been as one when he authoritatively started working for the FBI, there was most likely in her brain that he'd been a tremendous advantage for the association. He has a place here. Everybody being respected wasn't from the digital security division, however Chad still appeared like he had a place with this gathering of individuals.

Whatever is left of the night passed by superbly, and Whitney was happy Chad had chosen to go to the Custom-made Complexity dispatch party. Indeed, even along these lines, she couldn't shake the failure that after the gathering, Chad would be going to Lake Charles, and she would be staying in Sulphur.

Their rooms were on the same floor of the stupendous inn settled between a few extensive structures in downtown Sulphur. The stroll down the long lobby to their rooms positioned only a couple of entryways away appeared to take for eternity. Whitney wasn't certain what ought to happen next.

"I had an awesome time today," she said when they'd touched base at her entryway. Seeing him in a Harris suit and tie had been bringing on a surge of yearning to surge through her throughout the night. According to the thankful way he was gazing an opening through her exquisite blue trim dress, the inclination was shared. She'd swooped her hair to the side so that her thick Harris twists fell around her shoulder.

"I couldn't have become during this time without you close by."

"It was my pleasure. All things considered, you helped me out as well." Other than the incidental kiss, Chad hadn't made out of here her. They hadn't discussed what might happen once he did a reversal to Lake Charles, and she kept on working in Sulphur, however Whitney was certain of one thing. In the event that this was the last time she would invest quality energy with Chad , she was certainly going to make the most of it.

"I have a jug of wine chilling in the cooler. Might you want to have a night top?"

He looked a few doors down at his room before glancing back at her. "I don't have the foggiest idea, Whitney. I think its best that I come back to my room."

"Why?" she requested that attempting not sound excessively disillusioned. His alluring eyes turned upward and down her body, just ceasing when he landed back to her face.

"I've figured out how to be deferential, yet in the event that I go into your room, I don't think I'll have the capacity to hush up about my hands."

She murmured as she inclined toward her shut entryway. This was Chad , the main kid she'd kissed. The principal kid she'd cherished. She needed him more now than she'd ever needed anything.

"Your hands were made to be on my body," she said delicately. He stuck her with a penetrating gaze as her words waited noticeable all around. The first occasion when she'd said those words to him had been just before she'd chosen to lose her virginity to Chad . He'd never forced her to have intercourse, so she'd known in those days that she required an approach to tell him that the time had come. She hadn't expected then that he'd totally demolish the considered engaging in sexual relations with whatever other man later on. For Whitney, there was just Chad and it generally would be.

"The late spring of 2007," he said in a voice loaded with yearning and need. His lips slammed on hers with a yearning that coordinated her own. Making brisk work of the slide key, they tumbled into the room and rapidly close the entryway.

"I've truly missed you," Chad said in the middle of kisses.

"I've missed you as well. More than you understand." He astounded her when he broke the kiss and inclined his temple against hers. They were both breathing sporadically, yet she couldn't have cared less. She recollected the day she'd told Chad that at whatever point he inclined his temple against hers, she felt like their souls associated in a way they hadn't some time recently. It sounded gooey, however she'd implied it, and obviously, he'd recalled.

Chad drove them to the bed, untucking his shirt and uprooting his tie. Whitney commenced her heels and unclipped her hair, daintily shaking out her twists.

"You were constantly delightful," Chad said as he slid the straps of her dress off her shoulders. "In any case, now, there's this hotness about you that has been making me long to be inside you since you appeared at my doorstep."

When she was left in just her blue ribbon bra and undies set, she offered Chad some assistance with removing whatever is left of his garments. Her fingers were flimsy as she unfastened whatever remains of his shirt and evacuated his white undershirt. She ran her fingers over his characterized abs before moving to the clasp of his jeans. When she got to the zipper, she looked at him as she slipped her fingers into his boxers to glass him. His rascal was moment, and he let out a moan that made her shudder. He became harder in her grasp as her strokes became bolder.

"Not happening," he said, pushing her hand away and energetically hurling her on the bed. "I've been envisioning what was underneath your dress throughout the night. Since I've seen this inviting unmentionables, all I need to do is take it off."

His gifted fingers unfastened her bra inside of seconds. She lifted her hips off the bed as he gradually dragged her underwear down her thighs, marking her with another extreme gaze before he remained from the quaint little inn his eyes over all aspects of her stripped body.

"Stunning." He might have just voiced single word, however there was such a great amount of feeling in his tone, she could scarcely stand it. Her eyes took after his developments as he uprooted his boxers and hurled them to the side of the room.

Benevolence. Twenty-three-year-old Chad Harris had been great. Twenty-seven-year-old Chad Harris was out and out delectable. She constrained herself to swallow and attempted her best to advert her eyes to his face yct she proved unable.

"Entrancing," she whispered.

"I'll take it," he said with a snicker before ensuring them both and going along with her on the bed. He flicked her areolas in a trap that dependably got her wet in seconds before embedding a finger into her center to test her availability.

He guided into her with a moderate push, spreading her legs encourage separated the more profound he got. Her back lifted off the bed when his whole length was implanted in her glow. "I've missed this inclination."

A grin crossed his lips. "I've missed this as well. It's been a while for me."

"Me as well." She apprehensively bit her base lip. "Four years to be correct."

"Four years?"

She gestured her head. "Yes. I haven't been with any other individual."

"Poop, Whitney. It's now taking my entire existence to make this keep going to the extent that this would be possible, yet you can't say stuff like that and anticipate that me will be a man of his word."

"I never requesting that you be a man of his word in the room. I just ever needed you. The genuine you. The crude you."

All beguilement left his face, and was supplanted by a possessive look that cautioned her that he was done keeping down. Ownership was assuming control, and before the night was over, she was certain Chad Harris would satisfy each longing she had.

Chapter Seven

Chad didn't think he'd ever seen anything as delightful as the morning sun throwing a delicate shine over Whitney's exposed body. Regardless he recalled the first occasion when he'd looked at Whitney. In those days, her twists had been maneuvered into a high pig tail, and they were both in their pre-teenagers. His auntie, Simone, had educated him that he would have some help that late spring around the B and B. The minute Whitney had strolled into the B and B with her dad, he'd been confused. He hadn't seen a young lady look so immaculate and sweet. As they began cleaning his close relative's storm cellar, they'd become friends instantly. Soon thereafter, he inquired as to whether he could visit her each mid year, and in the end, Tyler went along with him as well.

A few years prior, his sibling had inquired as to whether he ever thought he would discover a lady he'd need to spend whatever is left of his existence with. Chad hadn't addressed and figured Tyler had definitely known the answer in any case. He'd met his future wife when he was twelve years of age. They might have become diverted the path, however there was most likely in his brain that she was his future. Presently, he simply needed to trust she felt the same.

He heard his telephone ding, flagging that he had another email message. He knew he needed to react to his old manager soon, however he needed to converse with Whitney first.

She balanced her position from her side to her back, giving him a far better perspective of her body. Not able to oppose, he trailed a solitary finger from the criminal of her neck down to the center of her bosoms and stomach, ceasing at the patch of the heaven he'd gotten acquainted with the previous evening. Moving rapidly with the goal that she wouldn't wake up, he balanced himself in the middle of her legs and spread her thighs sufficiently only to dunk his tongue into her sweet focus.

Her eyes opened restful, and her light groans immediately filled the room as she neared her enthusiastic discharge. Regardless she had the same sweet taste that had offered him some assistance with getting through a considerable measure of unpleasant times consistently. When her shivers started to die down, she went after him and maneuvered him into her grip.

"Great morning to you as well, Chad."

Chad had never been awesome at communicating his feelings, however it never appeared to trouble Whitney. Laying on the overnight boardinghouse her as firmly as he could without pulverizing her made him feel invigorated-allowed to dream about the future without being agonized over baffling his dad's memory. He nearly felt regretful to be this content with his dad never again arriving, however Chad was understanding that he'd spent the most recent year of his life stagnant since he'd passed. It was the ideal opportunity for that to change.

***

After thirty minutes, Whitney wasn't astonished that despite everything they stayed in bed interweaved in each other's arms.

"There were such a large number of times that I contemplated calling you," he said, at long last breaking their grip to investigate her eyes. "I hadn't understood, at the time, the genuine reason that I never pursued you the night we separated. I knew I wasn't the kind of man you required."

"I comprehend what you mean," Whitney brushed his cheek with the back of her hand. "After we separated, I understood I had a considerable measure of developing to do myself, and I couldn't be the sort of lady you required in the event that I didn't live for myself and not my dad."

"Surmise we both had a considerable measure of developing to do," he said with a giggle.

"We did." She grinned before becoming genuine once more. "It was clear at the function the previous evening that you adored what you did, and they clearly see your capability to develop in the digital security field. Things being what they are, would you say you are going to let me know why you haven't came back to the FBI?"

"You definitely know why."

"Due to your dad?"

"Yes," he said, inclining toward his back. "I might have frustrated the old man when he was living, yet now that he's gone, I can't keep on being a failure."

She twisted into his side and set her head on his mid-section. There weren't numerous things that astonished Whitney, however reviving a past relationship was certainly not what she thought would've happened a week ago.

"Initially, I exited the FBI in light of the fact that my father was biting the dust. Tyler and I had talked, and I guaranteed him that I would spend father's last days close by. I ensured father got the opportunity to do as much as he could before he passed. At that point, when it was the ideal opportunity for me to come back to work, I felt regretful about coming back to a calling that he never endorsed of."

"Blame is a monstrous monster."

"Let me know about it," he said with a constrained snicker. "It can expend you... in the event that you let it."

She lifted her head to his. "You can't carry on with your life for your dad. I comprehend why he was angry about the FBI, yet you aren't your dad. What's more, just in the event that you are worried about how you'll be as a father, I know you aren't anything like your mom either. FBI work or not, you'd never leave your crew."

He looked uncertain as he voiced his next words. "I left you four years prior."

"We left each other."

"How about we not do that once more."

His eyes were loaded with a guarantee that made her vibe confident. Following quite a while of thinking about whether she'd met Chad excessively youthful, on the off chance that she'd begun to look all starry eyed at him too early, she at long last recalled how it felt to trust and dream about the likelihood of until the end of time.

Chapter Eight

"In the event that you continue gazing at her such as that, individuals might begin about your expectations," Josie said.

Chad looked at Josie before giving back his look back to Whitney who was organizing at the dispatch party. He was happy that Josie and Rick were additionally in participation to bolster Whitney. The response from the gathering of people when they uncovered the Custom-made Modernity site and application was spectacular, and individuals were at that point giving him business cards. He wouldn't have much time for side work however. He as of now had a customer rundown he needed to keep up before preparing another person to handle the work load.

"Perhaps I need everybody here to see precisely what my expectations are, particularly every one of the men who appear to be energetic to stand out enough to be noticed today evening time."

"Who are you and what have you finished with Chad Harris?"

"Point the finger at it on Whitney. In one week, she's as of now flipped around my reality... Positively."

Josie giggled. "Man, who are you joking? Whitney's had that impact on you since we were children." Whitney pick that minute to stare at him and grin in a way that no one but he could decipher.

"According to the way you both continue taking a gander at each other, you've at last chosen to get back together."

"Despite everything I'm taking a shot at it." He hadn't conversed with Whitney, however he would when he got an opportunity to force her away.

"All things considered, I should discover my life partner, and you at long last have a discussion with my cousin about your relationship. Possibly our wedding won't be the one and only one year from now."

Chad scarcely heard Josie's last words. He was at that point making a beeline for Whitney. Losing her once had been the most troublesome a great time. Losing her a second time wasn't an alternative.

***

Her heart was pulsating out of her mid-section as Chad advanced over the space to her. She realized that walk. She realized that look. He had something at the forefront of his thoughts that he needed to examine with her, and when he looked that decided, putting off the discussion wouldn't happen.

"You better stamp your name on that one."

"What?" Whitney asked looking at Summer Jones, 33% of the Exposed Complexity Jones sisters.

"Chad Harris, that is the thing that." Mid year motioned to him. "He's clearly coming here for you, and his eyes have been stuck to all of you night. In the event that a man that looked as delightful as Chad, was gazing at me throughout the night, the last place I would be is at a gathering brimming with ladies holding up to jump on him."

"Be that as it may, I can't leave," she said, shaking her head. "I'm the Online networking Operations Director for Custom-made Complexity, so I'm certain Carla and Brad need me to stay until the end of the gathering."

"Sweetie, trust me. I will tell my sister that you couldn't stay and became ill or something. If not for you and Chad, we wouldn't have the capacity to have this gathering today evening time."

Chad welcomed Summer when he drew closer before inquiring as to whether they could talk.

"She can talk," Summer replied, introducing ceaselessly. "Truth be told, she can leave the gathering all together. I'll take care of everything."

Whitney didn't miss the wink Summer gave her as she got her jacket and took after Chad out of the gathering.

"I was contemplating sitting on that seat, however it's somewhat crisp out." She took after the course he was taking a gander at.

"That is fine. Sulphur dependably is by all accounts crisp during the evening, particularly since we're downtown by the lake. We can stay there."

When they sat down, Chad appeared to get anxious. "Is everything OK?"

"I have to ask you something."

"Alright. What is it?" She turned her body with the goal that she was confronting him on the seat.

"This previous week has been one of the greatest weeks I've had in years, and I don't need it to end."

"Me neither one of the she's," said with a grin.

"I landed another position offer from the FBI. There's a squad in the Sulphur office that is committed to digital wrongdoings and assaults. It's a prominent position and not the same as what I had done some time recently, so it will require infrequent travel."

"That so incredible, Chad !" She hung over to give him a snappy embrace. "I knew something was blending by how they were conversing with you at the recompenses function."

"I was shocked by the offer, and I need to acknowledge it however that relies on upon you."

Whitney squinted her eyes in disarray. "Why does it rely on upon me?"

Chad turned on the seat with the goal that they were confronting each other and took her hands in his.

"Whitney, I can't envision not having you in my life. When I'm with you, I'm a superior man, and you comprehend me superior to anything anybody I've ever known. I adore the way that I can give you a basic look, and you know precisely what I'm considering. I shouldn't have given you a chance to leave my life years back, and I decline to give you a chance to leave it once more. On the off chance that I accept this occupation, it will be a choice that we both make since I need to fabricate a future with you. I cherish you, Whitney, and in the event that you'll have me, I'll spend whatever remains of our lives demonstrating that our adoration is the sort that will last."

Exactly when Whitney was certain her heart couldn't develop any more for Chad , he figured out how to say the sweetest thing that she'd ever heard. "I adore you as well," she said grinning from ear to ear.

"You've effectively invested a lot of energy not doing what you cherish along these lines, obviously, I need you to accept the occupation. We can make sense of everything else together."

He flashed her a diminished grin. "I think its best in the event that I move to Sulphur since you're as of now building an existence here, and now, my employment will be here as well. In any case, I need to keep the house in Lake Charles with the goal that we can have a spot to stay when we're there. We can lease it out when we're not utilizing it."

Knowing Chad and in addition she did, she knew the implicit thinking behind him needing to keep his home in Lake Charles, Louisiana. They'd met in Lake Charles, begun to look all starry eyed at in Lake Charles, and revived their affection in Lake Charles. The house would be more than a spot for them to escape to when they needed to make tracks in an opposite direction from enormous city living. It spoke to their past, present, and future.

"That sounds flawless," she said as she inclined in for a kiss. When their lips touched, Chad pulled her closer, kissing her with more energy than he ever had some time recently. Following quite a while of feeling like her association with Chad was stopped as well, it appeared the stars were at last adjusting at the ideal time. The minute was so excellent, it actually blew her mind.

***

As time wore on, the townspeople gathered at the historical center in my town. It was an enormous old chateau with a truly pretty garden. The genuine wedding was set in the patio nursery under an one of those minimal curve things with pink roses all entwined in it. A white rug paved the way to the curve and when the blossom young lady strolled down, she hurled pink flower petals. Also, when they kissed, birds with pink strips attached to their feet were be released.

At that point, the gathering was inside in the dance hall place. The wedding part sat at the back on one of those long tables and other people were lounging around the room on round tables with white table garments and pink blossoms in the center. All the plates and utensils sparkled like precious rubies.

There was a lot of dancing and elegant music playing. Everyone did all the customary stuff like father and little girl move, hurling the bouquet, and so forth.

And after that they rode away in a white convertible with a major crude "Simply Married" sign on the back.

The End

Irresistible

Chapter One

The wind blew tenderly blending the leaves on the oak trees as a little gathering of individuals accumulated at the gravesite to say their last farewells to Joe Smith, a man known not one of the best criminal legal counselors in Lake Charles. His passing was sudden; a pile up on his route home from the courthouse at 38 years of age and things were never the same.

A lady wearing a dark Chanel dress laid a solitary red rose on his pine box as the minister read from the book of scriptures. She was youthful and amazingly excellent, with dim hair, eyes light cocoa and a solid jaw that talked about a determination to push aside any sentiments of misery or annoyance for the arrangement managed to her by the death of her better half.

Cassie and Joe Smith had been hitched for a long time; dated for three preceding that. A large portion of their companions would depict them as upbeat, perfect; perfect partners figuratively speaking yet for Cassie, Joe was her one genuine romance and following quite a while of euphoria, Cassie had brought forth a child young lady; Arianna.

Cassie swung to take a gander at their girl who remained alongside Joe's mom holding her hand. She was radiant in somewhat dark dress lined with a pink silk lace and her most loved pink shoes. Arianna had dependably been the dear of the house and Joe ruined her awfully with endowments and everything a young lady could need. Cassie was apprehensive as she strolled back to remain with her girl. Her relative looked at her and offered a grin despite the fact that they both knew the other was coming apart inside.

"Mama, is daddy going to be alright without anyone else's input? asked Arianna, gazing toward her mother with eyes wide and befuddled. Cassie's heart dove. How would you disclose to a three year old that her daddy isn't going to know's only he or even feel anything until kingdom come.

Cassie bowed before her and ran her hand through her hair. "Ari, recollect that I let you know daddy's going to paradise, isn't that so? He won't be separated from everyone else for long. There'll be blessed messengers with him". She gazed toward Joe's mother for help.

"I should take you back to the auto and sit tight for mother there? said Gwen removing her hand and driving Arianna from the graveside. Cassie mouthed a thank you and watched with tears in her eyes as her little girl left.

The minister completed the administration and everybody left in the wake of saying farewell one last time to the man who had touched such a large number of lives with his consideration and empathy. Cassie saw a man remaining over by the oak tree watching the administration from a separation.

He looked ambiguously natural yet then so did a large portion of the general population

at the gravesite. Cassie wasn't certain why yet his nearness

alarmed her. She dismissed and centered her consideration on leaving and home with her girl and Gwen who was staying with them for a couple days. They were holding up in the auto quietly and when she got in, the driver hurried away.

Their home was on a tranquil road lined with oak trees and a wonderful park over the route for the children to hang out on weekends and occasions. Joe took Ari there on weekends when he wasn't occupied with a case or away on business. It was their little bit of heaven and Cassie delighted in those minutes also. They made a great deal of recollections there throughout the years.

Cassie's eyes got obscured with tears as she battled the recollections of her late spouse. They escaped the auto and strolled as one to the front entryway. Gwen drove Ari inside as Cassie went upstairs to the room to change her outfit. When she returned, Gwen and Ari were making sandwiches in the kitchen.

"Mother, I made you a ham and cheddar. Grandmother helped me make it" said Arianna as her mother showed up. She pushed the plate over the counter and grinned at her mother.

Cassie brought the plate and sat down. "Thanks nectar. Perhaps later you and I can nestle up in my informal lodging read to you"

Arianna's grin lit up. "Would you be able to peruse the one about

the pixie? Daddy enjoyed that one best"

"I can do that" Cassie unsettled her hair and kissed her cheeks. "Gwen, I think perhaps after Ari's snoozing you and I can talk. There are a couple of things I need to talk about"

Gwen gestured accordingly and ate peacefully as Cassie and her little girl discussed minor stuff. She looked as they ate, pondering her child and the amount she missed having him here. He was the remainder of her two children to kick the bucket. His sibling David had passed on at a quarter century age from an extreme instance of endocarditis and to lose Joe too was a gigantic burden to manage. Gwen wasn't as solid as everybody thought except she put on a courageous face and held it together for her little girl in law and Ari.

"Gwen, would you say you are alright? Cassie asked, concerned she wasn't doing as such well. She generally attempted to stow away when something wasn't right yet Cassie knew she was continuing something back. At 70 years of age, Gwen had endured a few misfortunes throughout her life including her better half two years back, so Cassie stressed that Joe's passing would wear her out.

"I'm not as eager as I thought" she answered, pushing her plate aside. "I think I'll clean up and a short rest"

"If it's not too much trouble let me know whether you require me" Cassie offered, looking as she left. Ari completed her sandwich and left to go viewed the television in her room. Cassie was l eft alone to manage her sentiments; something she attempted to avoid. It was still excessively agonizing after the sum total of what Joe hadn't been dead for two weeks and years of recollections and affection couldn't simply vanish.

A few hours after the fact, Gwen thumped on Cassie's room entryway. Ari was snoozing next to her subsequent to having listened to her mother perusing the pixie sleep time story. She motioned for Gwen to come in.

"I needed to hold up until Ari was snoozing before we talked" said Gwen. "I've been intending to converse with you for some time however there never appear to be the opportune time". This sounded genuine.

Cassie settled her girl under the spreads and set the book down. "Is everything OK with you?

Gwen shook her head and the tears started to fall. "I have covered two children and a spouse, I'm not certain what alright ought to feel like. I needed to let you know that I'm going home tomorrow" She held up a hand when Cassie started to challenge.

"I adore you and Ari however I have to go home. A lot of Joe is in this house and I can feel him all over the place I turn. It's excessively"

Cassie went after her hand. "It's hard for me as well however having you here has helped me these previous few days. I wish

there was more I could accomplish for you"

Gwen shook her head. "You have done what's necessary and I will dependably be here on the off chance that you require me, you realize that"

They represented a few minutes before resigning to bed. Her flight was not until early afternoon so Ari had room schedule-wise to say farewell. It wouldn't be simple however they would survive this as well; Cassie thought as she floated off to rest.

Part Two (a few weeks after the fact)

Cassie wearing Levis and shirt to take her little girl out to the recreation center for some recess. She had been approaching to go throughout recent days however Cassie wasn't peaceful up to it. She held up persistently as Ari snatched her most loved toys and ran pass her mama at the front entryway.

She limited down the strides, skipping along the asphalt as Cassie took after firmly behind. She felt herself grin as she watched her daughter getting a charge out of the basic joy of being outside. It felt like perpetually since Cassie had been outside; most days she would scavenge through Joe's things attempting to deal with them. It would be another couple of days before she came back to work at the display and after that Ari would be back at childcare with her companions. She should have been around different children; to feel ordinary once more.

They achieved the recreation center without a moment to spare to see Hannah and her mother, Jessie. Hannah was Ari's companion from childcare. Cassie looked as they circled the recreation center kicking at the ball.

"Hey Cassie" said Jessie as she sat next to Cassie on a seal. "How are things with you?

"I am holding up decently well for Ari" she answered. "I'm backtracking to work one week from now so she'll be in childcare with Hannah. I would lean toward on the off chance that she was at home with Gwen yet she cleared out a couple of weeks back"

Jessie secured her hand with hers. They were dear companions and she could tell Cassie was concerned.

"She'll be alright, I guarantee. Kids have a method for skipping back like nobody can what's more Ms. Peterson watches them like a bird of prey"

Cassie giggled at the depiction yet it was fitting. Ms. Peterson was the manager at the childcare and a gift to a significant number of the guardians who experienced considerable difficulties great help.

They spent one more hour talking before Cassie needed to take off. She was drained and it was getting dim.

"Ari, it's a great opportunity to go. Say farewell to Hannah" she said. "It regarded see you Jessie. I'll make certain to have you and Hannah over soon".

"I'll call you" answered Jessie as she excessively arranged, making it impossible to go home.

Cassie lifted Ari and strolled to short separation home. They had turkey sandwiches for supper and not long after Ari nodded off. Cassie gave and dressed for bed, laying close to her little girl and considering what's to come.

She made arrangements to visit with Gwen in a couple of weeks however separated from that she had no different arrangements but to come back to work. Going back spoke to her; it was forlorn and miserable being at home throughout the day and it would be useful for Ari as well. Killing the lights, Cassie cuddled nearer

to Ari and nodded off.

A few days passed by rapidly and Cassie was up making breakfast for Ari before leaving for work. Grain and drain with organic product would suffice today as she had slept in and it was just about time to go.

They sat at the breakfast bar and ate; Ari spilling drain everywhere on her dress.

"How about we get you tidied up sweetheart" said Cassie walking her to the room. "We should get you into this". She held out a pink and white bounce suit with little bunnies on the pockets.

She immediately dressed Ari and subsequent to locking up the house, Cassie headed to the childcare a few pieces away. Ms. Peterson met them outside and after a fast word and a kiss, Cassie headed out. She battled back the inclination that Ari wouldn't be okay knowing Ms. Peterson would take great consideration of her.

A couple of hours after the fact at work, Cassie had a surprising visitor. Another executive of acquisitions was beginning today and her supervisor needed her to work with him. Nick Brady had a notoriety for being heartless and an eye for quick ladies. Cassie prepared herself for what might presumably be an uneasy first meeting. Before she could get up from her work area, a man dress immaculately in a dim suit strolled into

her office.

"You should be Cassie" he said taking the freedom to utilize her first name. He extended a hand to her which she won't. Cassie effectively decided not to like him.

"Mrs. Smith" she said, "I'm Mrs. Cassie Smith. I don't offered authorization to utilize my first name Mr. Brady".

He had the nerve to grin and sat down before her work area. "My statements of regret, It's my method for comforting you however I will forgo doing at such later on".

Cassie sat down and folded her legs. "I take it you and I are to cooperate so perhaps we ought to set some guidelines"

Nick sat back and grinned. He could enlighten she heard the bits of gossip concerning him; it would represent her standoffish conduct. He let it slide this time.

"OK Mrs. Smith. I'll listen to you". He respected a lady who held fast and when that lady looked as delightful as Cassie did, he was willing to humor them.

"In case we're going to cooperate, you ought to know I don't date my supervisors or associates it is possible that" she began. "My own life is beyond reach as is yours. For whatever length of time that you stick

to that we ought to be fine cooperating"

"Until further notice, I will acknowledge your terms. Presently should we start? he asked ascending from the seat. "Carlos might want us to begin by going once again the rundown of late acquisitions and have them assessed at the soonest time conceivable"

Cassie tailed him out and shut the entryway. They worked one next to the other for the following couple of hours going over the craftsmanship pieces and by twelve Cassie was drained. Her first day back was a touch of overwhelming. Her psyche was on Ari a fraction of the time and she was scarcely ever mindful of what she was doing as a less than dependable rule.

Nick saw yet said nothing of it. He knew through Carlos that she had as of late covered a spouse and lived alone with her three years of age little girl. While he knew they needed to complete the majority of the occupation today, he proposed they enjoy a reprieve.

"What about lunch? he inquired. "I know an awesome bistro only a couple obstructs from here. We could walk"

Cassie shook her head. "Apologies, the tenets recollect"

"This isn't a date simply lunch" he expressed. He felt the inclination to know her; needed to comprehend why she felt the should be so chilly towards him. Most ladies seized the opportunity to bed him immediately. He was after each of the an extremely nice looking lone wolf, tall dim and brandished the assemblage of Adonis.

Nick Brady was the encapsulation of a playboy and he

knew the notoriety that he had. Perhaps at one point in his life he had merited it yet after an unfortunate undertaking a couple of months prior, Nick changed riggings. His lesson had been learnt.

Cassie ascended from her seat and got her pack. "I'll see you around. I have a few errands to run". He looked as she left the room in a flurry. Nick was starting to see why he was pulled in to her. It wasn't simply physical, she was savvy and modern not at all like the majority of his old success. Cassie Smith would be an intriguing test.

In the mean time Cassie had lunch alone at Rick's, a little eatery not a long way from the exhibition. She knew the proprietor well and felt safe here. She required natural things throughout her life to keep from separating. Ari required her mother to hold it together for them both.

Rick, the proprietor strolled over to say greetings. "So your back at work. Heard there's another executive of obtaining; Nick Brady"

Cassie wasn't astounded; Rick knew things even she didn't think about.

"You know him?

Rick shook his head. "I know of him. His most recent sweetheart was a companion of a companion and i know it didn't end well. I

heard he..."

Cassie held up a hand before Rick could say any more.

"His own life is not my issue to worry about, Rick and I'd rather it remained that way"

"I can't point the finger at you" said Rick, He stood and gave her a thoughtful look. "Make certain not to succumb to this person however. I'd prefer not to see you wind up like whatever is left of them"

Cassie shrugged at his remark and completed her serving of mixed greens. She had no enthusiasm for men and perhaps she never would again. Who would ever coordinate up to Joe?

Cassie came back to the workplace and got done with dealing with the craftsmanship pieces. Brady was tied up in a meeting with the board so she was distant from everyone else in the workplace.

She was so made up for lost time in completing the employment, Cassie scarcely saw the time. A thump on the entryway shocked her back to reality.

"I figured you were a diligent employee yet it's way pass 4pm and unless you anticipate resting here which I know you don't" said Nick remaining in the entryway with his coat behind him. "You ought to get going. Your little girl is holding up"

"You're correct. It's late" Cassie got her coat and sack. "I didn't understand the time. I'll see you tomorrow"

"Tomorrow then, Mrs. Smith".

Cassie headed to the childcare and grabbed Ari, who was sleeping. At home, Cassie tucked her in overnight boardinghouse, changing into shorts and a shirt. She ate a chicken serving of mixed greens while understanding her messages. There were a few from old companions sending their sympathies however she disregarded those. She was excessively drained, making it impossible to consider what she had lost; her need now was to make life agreeable for Ari and herself.

Chapter three (after three weeks)

Nick woke early and went on five mile run to clear his head. He experienced considerable difficulties the previous evening and he knew Cassie was at fault for that. She filled his each idea and working with her was going to demonstrate troublesome.

He was pulled in to her yes however he likewise knew she would not like to have any kind of kinship with him outside of work. He expected to endeavor to get at her on the off chance that he'll ever get an opportunity to check whether she could have a change of heart.

However, he held a mystery that could smash any trust of that incident so Nick needed to play his cards right. He returned home and gave; prior breakfast. He and Cassie had a great deal to do today; Carlos needed the workmanship pieces completely evaluated and prepared for presentation by one week from now.

He landed at work ahead of schedule to discover Cassie officially working diligently in her office. She gazed upward as Nick drew nearer. She looked divine in a red dress that fitted her to flawlessness; indicating simply enough cleavage and her minor waist. Her hair superbly set up in a pixie trim that flaunted those immaculate cheek bones and impeccable skin.

Nick knew he was gazing however couldn't help himself. Cassie however was uncomfortable under his glare.

"Did anybody ever let you know gazing is rude, Mr. Brady? she inquired.

"Pardon me however i really wanted to notice how shocking you look in that dress"

Cassie disregarded the compliment and concentrate on the current workload; assessing a sketch Carlos had purchased from a well off old woman.

"I have a meeting with Carlos at ten and afterward I'm meeting with the top managerial staff" he educated her. "I'd like it in the event that you could go along with us"

Cassie turned upward from her work. "I must be in Suffolk this evening. Too bad"

Nick sat on the edge of her work area. "At that point we should eat to upgrade you on the most recent news. There will be some changes around here"

Cassie got up and strolled to the entryway. "I truly need to complete this today. Perhaps you can fill me on the meeting later". He knew when to take an indication; she needed to be allowed to sit unbothered.

Hours after the fact, Cassie sat in her auto in the parking area frantically attempting to begin the motor on her Camry with no luckiness. Of all the days to have an emergency, this was the most noticeably awful. Cassie had a meeting with Mrs. Vandermalt on the edges of town for a conceivable acquisition of two bits of stone carvers. She couldn't stand to be late.

A tap on her window startled Cassie. It was Nick.

"Auto inconvenience? he enquired of Cassie. "By what means would I be able to offer assistance?

She wasn't so certain tolerating his assistance was the most shrewd thing to do however innocuous it might appear.

"Mr. Brady, I value the offer yet I can call a workman. He'll be here right away" Cassie could swear she saw him attempting to conceal a grin.

He began to leave however then halted. Pivoting he said "May I offer to loan you my auto or else you'll be late for your meeting with Mrs. Vandermalt"

"I have room schedule-wise to arrive" said Cassie, snatching her handbag and hauling out a cellphone and began strolling.

"I understand you and I have become off in an undesirable manner, Mrs. Smith, however trust me when I say I'm just attempting to offer assistance".

Something in the way he said it made Cassie stop. Nick drew nearer her circumspectly.

"Ceasefire? he solicited dangling his keys in front from her. Cassie wavered only for a brief moment before grabbing them from his hands.

"I ought to be back in time for lunch" she said making a decent attempt not to grin. "Which auto is yours?

Nick indicated the silver Mercedes.

"I will monitor it with my life, guarantee".

After three hours, she was back at the exhibition and in great spirits. The meeting with Mrs. Vandermalt went well and not just did Cassie win her over with her appeal, the elderly and marvelously rich lady offered to be a supporter for the display.

This was a chance to grow the weath of the exhibition and make some vital associations. After all the Vandermalts were thee wealthiest individuals in the province. Cassie could barely hold up to impart the news to Carlos.

She strolled into her office and was astonished to see Nick there sitting tight for her.

"I thought you had a show today" said Cassie.

"One of alternate folks can deal with it. i needed to talk about the Vandermalt manage you".

It flabbergasted her how he knew such things. The arrangement was simply closed and Cassie hadn't told anybody at the display. Nick Brady was a secret.

"I should arrange in some lunch from the store up the road and we can begin"

'At any rate it wasn't a date' thought Cassie.

When she didn't question, Nick requested lunch for them

both and had one of the assistants lift it up.

They ate while examining the conceivable advantages of a support from the Vandermalt's lady and chose it was the best arrangement Cassie could have made.

"I think Carlos would concur with me when i give him the uplifting news" Nick said in the middle of chomps. "I'm awed with your work"

Cassie did whatever it takes not to grin. Nick was gradually developing on her regardless of the fact that she didn't remember it For a minute she thought they may really get along. It has been over a month since they met and the additional time she spent in his nearness, the more Cassie detected he wasn't the creature individuals made him out to be.

It was past four toward the evening and time to get Arianna from the childcare. Cassie smothered a yawn and moved to get her things together.

"I need to go. The auto is all great now, so here's your key" she said to Nick. "Much thanks to you such a great amount for this and the advance of your auto. I'll see you on Monday"

"It was my pleasure Cassie and might I recommend that you attempt the zoo this weekend" he said, perplexing her. "Your girl may appreciate the most recent expansion to the zoo; the new aquarium was simply opened"

However he shocked Cassie once more. She gave him one of her best grins.

"I'll consider it. I need to go". Cassie left, abandoning him remaining in her office. Nick had his very own arrangement, one that would definitely work to support him.

After a day, Cassie woke early and made breakfast for her and Ari; waffles and eggs, some new strawberries and juice. She was all the while considering where to take her girl to the zoo or possibly take a drive to the shoreline. It would be fun skipping in the sea and watching Ari make sandcastles. It was something she delighted in with her dad and something Ari had missed in the previous couple of weeks.

Cassie conveyed a plate up to her room where her girl lay dozing. She hung over and kissed her cheeks.

"Morning, sweetheart. Mama eats prepared" she advised her. Ari opened one eye and grinned at her mother.

"I have an astonishment for you today Ari" said Cassie. "How might you want to go see the new aquarium at the zoo? Hannah and Jessie could tag along"

"Can I swim with the fishes, mom? Ari asked honestly.

Cassie chuckled delicately and unsettled her hair. "No you can't yet I wager in case you're great today I can take you to the shoreline tomorrow".

Ari jumped up on the informal lodging here and there spilling the juice in the plate. Cassie was satisfied to see her so upbeat.

She went after Ari and set her down on the floor. "Go wash your face and hands and how about we eat". She looked as her little girl hurried to the restroom and gave back a couple of minutes after the fact.

They ate and watched kid's shows before Cassie left to call Jessie. She was happy for the day out and guaranteed to meet them at ten. Cassie had only two hours to get prepared.

Ari observed more kid's shows while her mother tidied up and paid some bills on the web. She looked at the clock and murmured. She had neglected to call Gwen. She generally did as such every Saturday morning.

Cassie dialed her number and held up.

"Hi" said the voice on the other side. She sounded somewhat drained.

"Hello there Gwen, it's Cassie" she answered. "Did I wake you?

"Really, you honeyed however don't stress over that" Gwen said. "How are you and my granddaughter?

"Ari is doing great as am I" Cassie answered then delayed. Something appeared to be peculiar. "Why are you in bed so late? It is safe to say that you are feeling okay?

She could hear her relative moan. Cassie became stressed with every excruciating moment.

"I have a little influenza, that is all" Gwen answered attempting to console her. "I'll be great in a matter of seconds, other than i require the rest. I'm not getting any more youthful"

That made Cassie much more stressed. Perhaps she required somebody to deal with her for a couple days. That gave her a thought.

"I think you ought to come visit with us for a couple days. Ari would love to see you and I would feel so much better having you here"

Gwen shook her head on the other side. She wasn't up to voyaging and frankly, she wasn't doing extremely well. Gwen didn't need Cassie to stress over her.

"I'll be fine Cassie. I have a companion staying with me so I'm not the only one. I have an arrangement to see Dr Spencer tomorrow so don't stress excessively".

It was getting late. Cassie had only a hour to get prepared and meet Jessie at the zoo.

"Guarantee to call me in the event that you require anything" she advised her relative. They said their farewells and hung up.

Cassie gave and wearing Capri shorts and a green top. Ari pick a purple pullover and shorts set and they were prepared to go.

Jessie and Hannah were at the door holding up pretty much as they had arranged.

"I purchased the tickets before to spare us some time" said Jessie, "as should be obvious, the line is entirely long"

"The whole district must be here today" Cassie watched. It would set aside a few minutes to see old companions and reconnect with them. Cassie hadn't made much time for delight since Joe had passed on. She was more overcome with dealing with her three years of age.

"How about we get moving then. I think we can begin at the lions. Ari cherishes them"

"That is an arrangement. How about we go young ladies" And off they went; the lions, bears, orangutans, giraffes were all dynamite and the children had a fabulous time. The passageway to the aquarium was marvelous with a curve route loaded with lovely sea animals swimming around. The entire aquarium was wrapped around them from roof to floor. There were a wide range of ocean animals however the whale shark was the most loved among every one of them.

"Ari and Hannah had some good times touching the glass and shrieking when the creatures swam too close. Pretty much as they were going to move away, a natural voice startled Cassie.

"I was trusting you would come". She swung to encounter Nick, shock kept in touch with everywhere all over.

"You had this arranged out isn't that right? Cassie asked, knowing this more likely than not been cap he needed. Inconvenience crawled into her voice.

"I don't blend work with family time, Mr. Brady". So they were back to that all things considered. He could tell she wasn't extremely satisfied yet he was tireless if nothing else.

"Nick. I lean toward on the off chance that you called me Nick, Cassie" he answered turning his regard for her girl. "You should be Arianna" He extended a hand to her which she took. He gave her a minishake.

"It is safe to say that you are mom's companion? she asked, her eyes wide. Ari was never anxious of outsiders.

Nick took a gander at Cassie. "We cooperated at the exhibition. Did you appreciate the aquarium?

"I like the whale shark, he's beautiful. Hannah likes him as well".

Cassie had overlooked her behavior. "Nick, this is my companion Jessie and her little girl Hannah. This is my supervisor Nick Brady"

Jessie grinned and shook hands with him. He was definately a catch and extremely great looking in dull pants and a white shirt. He noticed great as well.

Cassie stood and listened as they bantered. She was amazed to perceive how calm he was with the young ladies and they appeared to like him as well.

They strolled to alternate displays while Nick and Jessie hit it off. Cassie wouldn't fret by any stretch of the imagination, truth be told she trusted his consideration would remain focused. She focuesed her consideration on the creatures and taking photographs of the young ladies.

It was close to two toward the evening and the young ladies were getting ravenous. There was a little bistro close-by that made the best italian sandwiches and plates of mixed greens.

"We should get some nourishment into these minimal ones" Cassie proposed. "We can go crosswise over to Evita".

Nick took a gander at her and grinned. He had the mst even arrangement of teeth she had ever seen. "How abou i make this my treat? I haven't had since breakfast and i can without a doubt utilize the organization of four wonderful women"

Jessie become flushed; Cassie shook her head. Nick grinned as he watched Cassie response. He knew her well; she wasn't happy with him just yet in time he'll make certain to change that.

They continued to the bistro and requested sandwiches for the young ladies and plates of mixed greens for themselves. Nick watched Cassie as she conversed with Ari and was touched by how defensive she was.

He loved that about her; his own mom never treated him that way. He spent his life growing up with babysitters and all inclusive school; his instructors and companions were his family.

Nick had two siblings, Jonah and Brandon and they were close. Jonah lived in Spain and functioned as a therapeutic specialist while Brandon lived in New York and made his living on Wall Street as a money related consultant.

Their folks passed on years prior while on a contracted flight to Lisbon, Portugal. The senior Mr. Brady had arranged an exceptional outing to commend their commemoration however the plane never made it over the Atlantic. It collided with the sea and left the three young fellows stranded.

It was something Nick never talked about and in some ways he never missed his folks; after all he spent his life being raised by others. He and his siblings carried on with a decent life and they never underestimated each other.

"Nick? he heard Cassie say. he was so somewhere down in his considerations he had quit e ating with the fork most of the way to his mouth.

"I'm sad. I was simply considering something" he said apologizing. "What were you saying?

"I was telling Jessie how we simply persuaded an affluent supporter to be a promoter of the exhibition" said Cassie.

Nick looked at Cassie straight without flinching. "I merit none of the credit. Cassie's beguiling identity did it all. I'm extremely awed with her work"

Jessie saw the way he took a gander at her companion. It wasn't lost on her that Nick Brady enjoyed Cassie. Did she give back the feeling was something else and Jessie couldn't endure to discover.

Cassie shrugged and turn her consideration back to her little girl who was currently yawning. It was rest time.

"I've had enough for the day and Ari's drained" she said. "We're prepared to go home. Would you all like to stay a while longer? I wouldn't fret"

Jessie took a gander at Hannah. "I think we ought to retire until tomorrow and go. I need to drive up to Harbor Bay tomorrow" she answered. "My mother's having the whole family over for supper"

"I'll walk you to the auto".

Ari had nodded off so Cassie needed to convey her while Nick followed along not far behind. She had the inclination he was watching her derriere which made her uneasy. She was making a decent attempt not to pivot and face him.

"I'm happy to see you took my recommendation" said Nick. "Kids love this sort of stuff. I recall my babysitter would take my siblings and I to see the dolphin show at the aquarium

m. We had a ton of fun. Once Brandon fell into the pool and a dolphin swam up to him. He shouted so uproariously we couldn't quit chuckling. Fortunate for him, they are amicable animals"

They both roared with laughter. Cassie could picture the scene in her mind. She recalled what it resembled going on trips when she was youthful and despite the fact that it was frequently just Cassie and her mother, she had bunches of fun. They made it to the auto and Vanesa set Ari into the auto seat. She swung to face Nick.

"We should not blend business with joy" she reminded him. "So, a debt of gratitude is in order for offering to us and I 'll see you at work"

Nick gave a salute and smiled as Cassie shook her head and moved into the Camry. She looked at him before heading out. He was certain Cassie was warming up to him and all he needed to do was play his cards right.

Chapter four (a few days after the fact)

Cassie had the three day weekend and chose to take Ari for a play day at the recreation center. She was drained from working relentless on a presentation at the exhibition yet it was justified, despite all the trouble. It could get greatly required income to grow the business which was Carlos' fantasy.

Nick had proposed the display and after that a dark attach supper a while later to be held in the considerable lobby on the second floor of the building. She had literally nothing to wear and with the occasion only two days away, she had little time to shop.

Today however was just about her and Ari having some good times and no considerations of work or Nick who appeared to have crawled into her head as of late.

He had astounded her with a bundle of tulips the day after the trek to the zoo and afterward he had sent her a wicker bin of treats for Ari just yesterday. Cassie didn't know why yet he was doing decent things she never requested. Perhaps he was simply attempting to make companions however whatever his reason, Cassie was gradually beginning to like him.

IT was nearly twelve and Cassie was drained from sitting and watching Ari ride the see saw and play in the sand pit with alternate children. It was cool out and in spite of the fact that she delighted in the outside with Ari, Cassie required some rest. She literally needed to pulled her girl far from the sandpit kicking and crying.

Cassie resisted the urge to panic while managing her fit. She had gotten a touch of that of late from Ari; the loathsome three was getting the opportunity to be a drag yet it was a piece of parenthood. They strolled up the road and was all of a sudden mindful of an auto stopped before their home. Cassie perceived the auto; it was Nick'. She looked as he got out and inclined toward the entryway sitting tight for her.

"What are you doing here? she inquired. He had the nerve to grin at her.

"I was in the area and saw you all strolling from the recreation center. Howdy Arianna" he answered, twisting to make proper acquaintance with the her.

"Are you desiring lunch, Mr. Nick. I'm going to help mama heat treats" said Ari.

"What's your most loved sort. Mine's oats and raisins"

Ari grimaced. "I like chocolate chips" She swung to her mom. "Can he help us with the treats please?

Cassie never took her look from his face. "I'm certain Mr. Nick has preferred things to do over prepare treats and ...."

"Really I don't" he said intruding on her. He was more than willing to get his hand loaded with mixture just to invest some energy becoming more acquainted with her. "I would love to go along with you folks" He grinned and winked at Ari, taking her hand in his. "Lead the way Cassie".

This would have been torment. Cassie gave in and not long after them three were in the kitchen make batter for treats. Ari filled hers with chocolate chips and made a couple oats and raisin treats for Nick.

"You're okay at this" he said to Ari. "Did your mother show you how to make treats?

Ari shook her head. "My daddy demonstrated to me how. He's gone now" For a moment she looked truly tragic. "Mom said he's in paradise with the blessed messengers yet I need to see him"

Nick stooped to converse with her. "All things considered, my daddy and mama are in paradise as well, so I'm certain your daddy is alright. He can see you from where he is and you don't have stress over him"

Cassie watched the trade and stifled on a tear. It was sweet what he simply accomplished for Ari, uncovering his injuries like that yet it took a delicate and kind soul to do that for a tyke. She felt a recently discovered appreciation for him.

"Why not folks go out back and I'll put the treats in the broiler". She required a couple of minutes to get it together.

Nick drove Ari out the indirect access and into the fenced in

back yard where she had a swing set up. Ari roared with laughter as Nick pursue her over the grass lastly getting up to speed to her. He lifted her in his arms as she shouted. Cassie viewed from the window and grinned. It was decent to see Ari have a fabulous time regardless of the possibility that the man wasn't her dad. It was something Cassie knew her girl had missed in her life.

She put two sheets of treats in the broiler and went along with them outside. Ari was on the swing by then and Nick sat and viewed over her. Cassie sat close to him and stayed noiseless.

Nick Brady was ending up being a genuine man of honor, not at all like the man individuals guaranteed him to be. In what capacity would he be able to be the point at which he was so kind to her girl.

"Much obliged to you for giving me access your home" he said to her. "I understand you and I are not exactly companions just yet but rather I'm wanting to alter that"

Cassie giggled. "how would you proposed we do that? Your notoriety for being a womanizer is extremely overwhelming and I'm not entirely certain I like you"

Nick scowled. That announcement hurt.

"That is not exactly genuine however else you wouldn't have permitted me here" he answered. "We can begin by going to the supper as a date."

"No" Cassie reacted immovably. "You and i will do no such thing. We cooperate and consider what Carlos would think"

Nick swung to take a gander at her. "That is the reason you treat me with chilling disdain at work...because of Carlos? He loves the possibility of us. He even recommended i solicit you out a couple from times"

That was news. Carlos never meddled in his representative's issues. Cassie thought that it was difficult to trust him.

"I think the treats are done" she said and got up. Nick went to push Ari on the swing. He wasn't putting forth a decent defense for himself with Cassie. He needed to make sense of another procedure and quick as well.

In the interim, Cassie put the treats on a plate. Nick was making her apprehensive and it wasn't on the grounds that she discovered him appealing and sweet and ....

'Gracious god, I should lose my brain" she contemplated internally. Nick wasn't her write and even so she simply wasn't prepared for another relationship.

She watched out the window and called them in. "The treats are prepared" She gathered a sack for Nick.

"It was pleasant of you to help yet i think we ought to say farewell now"

Nick didn't take offense to it, he essentially took the sack and told Ari farewell.

"I'll see you tomorrow night" he said and strolled to his auto. He would need to compensate for it at the supper.

The following day, Cassie dropped Ari off at the childcare and went looking for a dress. She found the ideal dress at Coco's; a red strapless fit and flare ball outfit with ruching at the waist. It had a changed sweetheart neck area and she looked astonishing.

She paid for the dress and completed her hair and nails at the salon nearby. A few hours after the fact, Cassie was looking in the mirror at her appearance. She was lovely.

She heard an auto pull up outside and hunked its horn. Carlos had guaranteed to send an auto for her. She got her coordinating grasp and went outside.

At the supper, everybody looked pleasant in outfits and tuxedos. Nick spotted Cassie the minute she strolled through the entryways and his pulse went up a score. She felt his look upon her however disregarded it picking rather to blend among the visitor.

Cassie spotted Mrs. Vandermalt and advanced there. She in any event could give the required diversion Cassie needed from the all powerful eyes of Nick Brady.

Mrs. Vandermalt turned out to be an exceptionally clever and proficient lady; her scope of subjects extended from legislative issues to design to pretty much everything Cassie could comprehend. The elderly lady was developing on Cassie.

She could tell somebody was drawing closer and she required no eyes to advise her it was Nick. Cassie turned in the nick of time.

"Great night madam. You look as wonderful as usual" he said taking Mrs. Vandermalt's hand and planting a kiss there. He was smooth if nothing else.

The elderly lady grinned and tapped his cheek. "Nick, it has been ages since I looked at you" she said. "How are Jonah and Brandon when you last saw them?.

"Jonah stays in Europe, Brandon is right now in New York. I will let them know you ask of them" he answered, then turned towards Cassie. "In the event that you will permit it, I think Cassie is required else where"

Mrs Vandermalt gave a gesture and he offered his hand to Cassie, who took it meekly. They exited to the overhang where the group was little. The air was crisp and possessed an aroma similar to lavender. Cassie took a full breath to quiet her spirits.

"You don't should be startled of me Cassie" he said to console her. He could tell she was apprehensive.

"I am not apprehensive of you Nick. I am uneasy in light of the fact that I don't have any acquaintance with you all around ok and I'm not certain I can trust yo

u". She pivoted to watch out at the greenhouses. The perspective starting here was downright amazing.

"At that point how about we become more acquainted with each other. I can let you know anything about me you wish to know and in return you can do likewise" he advertised

Cassie answered "Alright then, let me know about your siblings. Is it true that you are close?

Nick snickered delicately. "We are truth be told. Jonah, he's the most established and a specialist in Spain. Brandon deals with Wall Street, a budgetary guide I'm the center tyke. Our folks are expired"

Cassie take a gander at him with that last piece of data. She too had lost her folks years prior.

"I have no kin and Joe, that is my significant other, passed on a couple of months back. Ari and his mom are my family" she said. "I have an auntie yet we aren't as close as we used to be"

Nick waved to the server for two glasses of white wine. He motioned for Cassie to sit.

"That wasn't so terrible was it" he said. "Presently we know something about the other, we can chip away at becoming acquainted with additional"

The server came back with the wine intruding on them. He gave a glass to Cassie.

She thought about his recommendation. It wouldn't hurt to

give him a chance to take her out once in a while however the length of it didn't get to more than that.

"I'll give you a chance to do your thing however under some conditions" she said. "I'll give you a chance to take me to lunch just once. I feel that ought to at least hold you under tight restraints for some time longer"

Nick knew it wouldn't however it was an offer he would not likely won't. Cassie had no clue what was in store for her.

He brought his glass up in a toast, Cassie took after.

"To the beginnings of a fellowship" he said. "Let me know one thing Cassie. What alarms you about me? I envision the gossip factory has been in overdrive since I came here and the stories are not as lovely as I trust"

She didn't answer simply then however took a couple tastes of the wine before talking. Cassie preferred to be straightforward regardless of the fact that it damage and this case it may.

"I heard you have particular talent with women and by way I don't mean anything great" she answered, confronting him straightforwardly. "You're known not canny, remorseless and malicious to the point where you seek after ladies and afterward suddenly leave their lives when you've bedded them"

That was new to Nick yet he listened without talking.

"I couldn't care less much for gossipy tidbits Nick yet I would prefer not to t

hink a man can be so chilly when it makes advances on the issues of the heart". So far he never showed those qualities to her. Nick was sweet with Ari so Cassie thought that it was difficult to trust that same man could be so barbarous. Still, she needed to tread circumspectly with this kinship.

Nick thought for a moment. Some of what she said had some truth to it however it was generally overstated. Yes, he has had what's coming to him of sentiments and dramatization however in all reasonableness, Nick could never treat his woman love coldly. It was forever his expectation to discover love yet the greater part of his victory were gold diggers camouflage as bona fide love interest and the moment he remembered this, it was over.

The Brady name had cash kept in touch with on top of it and ladies were attracted to that. He had intense associations that he seldom utilized and having his dad's great looks added to the catch. The siblings were a magnet for ladies and it had dependably been that way.

With Cassie, be that as it may, Nick felt distinctive. She was not put off by the gossipy tidbits but rather she wasn't bouncing into his bed either. Cassie captivated him; her grin, the way she held her little girl, the commitment she had for her work. She was solid but tender and he enjoyed her massively

They sat out on the overhang a couple of minutes more before coming back to blend with the group. Cassie found a couple of the supporters of the exhibition and drew in them in an exchange on the most recent of their acquisitions before withdrawing to the women room.

In the mean time, Nick invested his energy in the organization of Mrs. Vandermalt and another of her partners. It was becoming late and entirely soon he knew Cassie would clear out.

It was just about ten around evening time. Ari would be sleeping at this point yet Cassie became anxious. She was drained; making discussion with a few prominent individuals and a couple of Carlos' companions. The supper was a win and in the wake of eating opposite Nick for the most recent hour with him gazing eagerly at her, Cassie was prepared to go.

She was going to get into the auto when she felt a hand on hers.

"Leaving without saying farewell? he inquired.

"I need to get Ari. She's at Hannah's for the night" she let him know. "I need to go. I'll see you on Monday"

"At that point I won't keep you. Until then". He grinned and looked as the auto headed out.

Chapter Five.

Ari, would you be able to get your sack please" Cassie shouted. She had slept late in light of the fact that she had been up from a large portion of the night with a cerebral pain.

It was Monday and having two gatherings consecutive didn't improve the situation either. Cassie Smith was never late for work.

Ari hurried to the kitchen with her bag close by and completely wearing a yellow jumpsuit and shoes. Cassie stuffed her snacks and drove her out to the auto.

She headed to the childcare and in the wake of making proper acquaintance with Mrs. Patereson, Cassie headed to work. She was without a moment to spare as the meeting was going to be begin. She got a look at Nick at the leader of the table as she sat down.

After thirty minutes, the meeting was done and Cassie strolled to her office. She was caught up with recording some completed paerwork when Nick thumped on her entryway. He inclined toward it dressed perfectly in a white shirt and dark customized pants, his sleeve moved up.

Cassie imagined not to notice how nice looking he looked remaining there. She thought it was rude to her late spouse to think about another man that way. Joe had been

dead for just a couple of months afterall.

"What may I accomplish for you Nick? she asked while recording her

archives away. She didn't meet his eyes.

He stayed in the entryway. "I needed to check whether you were free for lunch today. There's an eatery three pieces from here that I 've never attempted. Is it accurate to say that you are amusement?

She promised him a get-together.

Cassie turned upward from her work area. "alright.. beyond any doubt. I figure I can eat."

"I'll come get you at twelve. I have around a hour prior to I need to meet with the executives this evening" he answered.

Cassie gestured and came back to her work leaving Nick to gaze at her. When she gazed upward a moment later he was no more. Cassie sat back in her seat and moaned.

'what am I to do with him' she pondered internally. Nick was influencing her only a little however in the event that she invested more energy with him, it will undoubtedly develop into something else. While Cassie wasn't against dating once more, she'd rather it be with somebody outside of work.

Her telephone rang simply then intruding on her considerations.

"This is Cassie" she replied. The number was unrecognized.

"Hello there Cassie. I'm calling from the City View Medical Center"

the voice on the other side said. It was a medical attendant. "Gwen Winter

s was conceded here a couple hour back and we have you on record as a closest relative"

Cassie stood and got her sack. "Is it true that she is alright? What was the deal?

The attendant attempted to reaasure her. "Mrs Smith was conceded for treatment of Pneumonia and dehydtration. She requesting that I call you"

"I'll be there in a couple of hours". Cassie hung up and raced to Nick' office. He was on a phone call however put it on hold when he saw the expression all over. He strolled around his work area.

"Cassie, what's going on? he asked, his voice tensed. He Arianna alright?

Cassie sat down and attempted to stay formed however tears undermined to fall. She took a full breath and talked.

"Joe's mother is in the healing facility and I need to go and see her" she let him know. "Can I have two or three days? i know things are kind of occupied now however she's the main other family I have and I ....."

Nick held up his hand. "You don't need to say much else. I can address Carlos and have something wokred out. Meanwhile, in the event that you give me the data, I can organize your flight and I think you'll need to take Ari as well".

Cassie was astounded yet by and by. This man considered everything. She was appreciative. Subsequent to giving him the data he required, Cassie left work and headed to the childcare focus.

Mrs'Peterson was staggered by the news. She knew Cassie must be concerned, having lost Joe months prior. She conveyed Ari to her mother and wished Cassie good fortune.

Back at home, Cassie gathered her packs and Ari's. Gwen lived in Waterford, a thirty moment battle from Lake Charles. She didn't have an arrangement however once she arrived Cassie would make sense of the rest. Joe's mother was her last connection to him; she should have been there for her.

After one hour Nick was at her front entryway. Cassie welcomed him in.

"I could get you and Ari on a flight for today evening time. You ought to be in Waterford by ten and an auto will lift you up and take you to the healing facility" he educated Cassie. "A companion of mine has prescribed a caretaker administration there so here's the number. You can have somebody watch Ari while you visit the healing facility"

Cassie took the paper he held out and said thanks to him. "I am thankful for your assistance and I'm truly sad about lunch" s he said. "Perhaps when things settle down?

Nick answered "We'll discuss that when you get back. I need to go now yet call me and let me know how everything is with your relative"

She strolled him to the entryway. "Much obliged again for your assistance"

"Whenever" he answered and left. Cassie shut the entryway and murmured with alleviation. She needed to get going on the off chance that she was going to catch her flight.

After two hours, she was at the airplane terminal and clearing movement. Ari was sleeping and Cassie breathed easy perusing a way of life magazine. Their flight was another thirty minutes away and when they at long last called for loading up, Cassie was drained and hungry.

The flight arrived at nine forty five that night and as guaranteed an auto was holding up at the airplane terminal with a babysitter for Ari. Nick was basically astounding.

The babysitter took Ari from Cassie and offered a thoughtful grin. She was appreciative and after a brief presentation and talk, the auto took them straight to City View Medical Center. The babysitter held up in the parlor with Ari while Cassie discovered Gwen's room.

She was in a private room off the medical attendants station. Gwen was sleeping however woke when Cassie put a kiss on her fore

head. She opened her eyes and was upraised to see Cassie.

"You came" she said in a voice that was so frail from being wiped out and tired. Cassie let a tear slip pass her watchman. She immediately wiped her face.

"Where else would I be? she teased smoothing ceaselessly the elderly lady's hair. She sat on the edge of the informal lodging her hands. They were icy.

"The medical caretaker let me know you have pneumonia however it's not as genuine as I thought" said Cassie, "you had me stressed for a moment"

"I didn't need you to worry. I thought it was only an influenza, I wasn't that wiped out a couple days back". Gwen was frail and dried out from days of a high fever and not eating much. She could have kicked the bucket.

Cassie stayed with her for a couple of minutes all the more then let her rest. She took Ari to Gwen's home and let the babysitter keep with it on the off chance that she needed to surge back to the doctor's facility. It was hard to rest so Cassie called Nick. It was practically midnight yet he addressed immediately.

"It's Cassie" she said. "I couldn't rest".

Nick could hear the exhaustion in her voice. "How is your relative? He sat up in the quaint little inn his eyes envisioning her in his brain.

"Gwen will be fine. She simply needs some rest and nourishment"

she let him know. "She's agony from parchedness and in addition pneumonia so her recuperate may take a couple of weeks"

That wasn't the news he expected yet Nick was eased to know it was nothing excessively genuine.

"I think I may bring her home with me when she's released from that point. Gwen needs somebody to take care of her"

"In any case, you can motivate somebody to tend to her there in her own particular home which is the thing that she may favor" Nick recommended. That seemed well and good. Gwen was strong-willed; she would like to be in her own particular home.

"I'll converse with her when visit tomorrow" she said, then recollected the caretaker. "Much obliged for the assistance. I couldn't have made do with Ari independent from anyone else at this moment. In any event she'll be here in the house and far from all the disease at the doctor's facility"

Nick grinned. He played his cards simply right. He knew the path to her heart may very well be to demonstrate he was prepared to do great; that the gossip she heard where only that; gossipy tidbits

They talked for a couple of minutes before Cassie floated off to

rest. Tomorrow she would begin once more.

Chapter Six

A couple days after the fact at the doctor's facility Cassie marked papers to discharge Gwen. The specialist concurred she was well enought to go home on the off chance that somebody would be there to help her. Cassie had enlisted a buddy/attendant for Gwen subsequent to counseling with her broadly.

She expressed gratitude toward the staff before having the chaperon wheel Gwen out the front entryway. Once at home, Cassie tailed her to the couch.

"I trust you're fulfilled by the medical attendant I discovered" said Cassie. you here. Marcy has my numbers and she'll keep me upgraded on your advancement".

Gwen feigned exacerbation. "Cassie sweetheart, I do love you so however I wish you would quit getting all worked up about me"

Cassie pulled a cover over Gwen. "I'm going to cook supper. Ari ought to be here any moment"

"Where is my excellent infant" Gwen asked glancing around. 'She 's out at the recreation center with Danielle, the caretaker Nichalos got for me. He's the new person at the display I let you know about".

"That was awfully decent of him however" answered Gwen, "You folks are truly close"

Cassie shrugged at that remark. She wouldn't characterize their relationship as close however they were not far off as they first were.

"I'm going to make you a fish pasta, would you like that?

"I'll eat whatever you make" said Gwen. Simply then Ari strolled in with the babysitter close by. She hurried to the couch and unto her grandmother's lap. It was a gathering Gwen savored and Ari was all giggles as she tickled her underarm.

Cassie cooked while viewing both of them reconnect. She was glad to have her relative home and safe so Ari could appreciate some time with her.

They had arrangements to leave in three days; Cassie needed to return to work and to her own life. She hadn't addressed Nick since that night yet he wasn't a long way from Cassie's idea. His generosity towards her and Ari had permitted her to see he wasn't as terrible as everybody thought.

They ate a hour later and Cassie resigned to bed leaving Danielle in control. Marcy wouldn't begin until Cassie left. Her telephone rang while she lay perusing a novel.

She knew it was Nick before she replied.

"Impeccable planning" she said, setting the book aside and cradl

ing the telephone nearer to her. She felt a glow inching through her at the sound of his voice.

He was simply getting prepared for bed when Nick chose to call her. They hadn't talked in days and he was missed her.

"How's beginning and end going at your end? he inquired.

"Gwen's back home and I employed a medical caretaker to stay with her" said Cassie, "she's doing as such much better so we ought to be back home this weekend"

Nick grinned at his end. "At that point possibly I ought to take you all ouy for supper or perhaps only a day at the shoreline"

"I may be excessively drained. Possibly you'll need to settle for simply lunch". Cassie owed him that much. Nick then again was baffled.

"I'll take that" he answered. "Would it be wrong in the event that I let you know I miss you? Cassie was shocked that it made her vibe needed.

"I think you ought to let me know what's happening at the display" she answered changing the subject. Nichols didn't push the issue yet rather did as she inquired. They discussed the most recent at the exhibition and it made Cassie miss work.

She looked at the clock; it was past ten. Cassie was drained and expected to rest. They said their farewells and soon toward the back

er she hung up, Cassie felt into a profound rest.

Friday came and the time had come to go home. Cassie was dismal to

leave Gwen however the medical caretaker was there now and she felt certain her relative would be alright.

After an uneven plane ride home, Cassie and Ari drove back to Lake Charles from the airplane terminal. The house was an appreciated site as Cassie drove up. Drawing nearer the front entryway, she saw a colossal bunch of red roses on her yard. Cassie recovered them and set them on the kitchen counter inside. There was a card on them.

Cassie knew they were from Nick before she opened the card. It read straightforward 'Welcome home'. Cassie set it aside and went after her telephone. It was getting to be harder to disregard him on the off chance that he continued doing things like these.

"I got your blossoms" she said once he replied. It was a lovely welcome home blessing. "I figure I owe you lunch"

Nick was grinding away and going to enter a meeting. "I'm happy you like them. Tune in, I'm heading into a meeting. Could I drop by later this evening?

Cassie thought for a brief moment. "Approve then. See you later". Jhours. Cassie felt anxious interestingly. She wasn't certain why however by one means or another Cassie knew things were slowl

y changing between them.

Ari came running into the kitchen. "Mama, would we be able to make

treats? i need treats for supper".

Cassie roared with laughter and lifted her in her arms. "Ari, you know treats are not for supper. I should make you

some chicken and pureed potatoes?

Ari scowled. She was determined to treats. Cassie attempted to locate a center ground. At that point she had a thought.

"We can make treats and have them for desert on the off chance that you have all your supper" she advised her little girl. "OK with that?

Ari gestured and squirmed out of her mother's arm, running out the secondary passage and into the yard. She was on the wilderness exercise center and cherishing it. Cassie began on supper and watched her little girl through the window. It all of a sudden struck her that she wasn't to Joe's graveside since he kicked the bucket. Without intending to, Cassie thought about her late spouse, possibly on the grounds that she felt regretful for continually being so solid and not separating for her misfortune.

It was odd that she would consider this when Nick was dropping by in a couple of hours. It would turn out to be a genuine discussion piece ought to Cassie constantly bring it up.

The odor of chicken took Cassie's recalled the present. She completed the potatoes and set them to bubble.

Supper was done thirty minutes after the fact and with a cluster of treats in the broiler, Cassie went along with her little girl outside.

They had a fabulous time playing on the swing and a little while later it was

time for supper and treats.

Ari completed up and excrement into the treats before her mother

could alter her opinion. Cassie let her have two then gave her a shower. They were sitting in front of the TV when the doorbell rang. Suspecting it was Nick, Cassie opened the entryway.

He ventured inside and planted a kiss on her cheek. Cassie shuddered and held up a hand to his mid - Chapter.

"Nick, I don't think..." she began yet he shook his head.

"I'm not attempting to tempt you" he said, He saw the look In her eyes. "Unwind, I needed to say hello there's nothing more to It. I brought something for you". He held out a little box wrapped with a bow.

Cassie opened her blessing and grinned. "Chocolate. You purchased me chocolate. How decent of you". She drove the path to the couch. Ari had gone upstairs to watch the TV in her room.

"Ari's upstairs. We can sit in here and talk" she signaled to the seat and sat at the inverse end. Nick drew a little nearer until he was sufficiently close for her to smell face ointment.

"You never addressed my inquiry" he said. Cassie was befuddled.

"Which one?

"In the event that it was suitable to let you know that I missed you"

Cassie took a gander at him. "Did you really? I don't comprehend what to let you know genuinely. I can't guarantee you anything Nic and I think you need me to"

He moved sufficiently near brush his hand against her cheek. "I missed you. I've been considering you consistently and it has been driving me insane".

Cassie couldn't take her eyes off him. She was in a daze; battling it.

"You're quiet is executing me Cassie" he proceeded. "Let me know what you're considering, what you feel"

She attempted to talk however the words got away from her. It was difficult to think when he was so close, so good looking and noticing the way he did. It was inebriating.

"Nick, I think you are sweet and i'm gratfeul for the times you've ventured into help and it's truly more than I ever expected of you" Cassie answered. "I can't imagine that I don't care for you...."

Nick put on a show to be irritated. "You wound my heart if

that is all i am to you. I think you need it to be something all the more yet you're perplexed"

Cassie moved further away yet he grasped her h

what's more, "Try not to flee".

She turned and confronted him. "I'm not apprehensive Nick at any rate

not of you".

"At that point what's the matter? he asked truly. He touched her face and looked for a response and pretty much as he expected, she shuddered at his touch. "You and I have science, we have something between us that has gradually assembled and I know you feel it as well and perhaps the planning is off or possibly it's simply right whichever way Cassie, i believe it's alright in the event that we attempt to see where it will take us".

"What's more, on the off chance that I can't? she inquired as to whether she could. "Imagine a scenario in which you and I can't go past today evening time, will you accet that.

Nick grinned. "I'm willing to attempt. I think anything is conceivable"

He gradually pulled her nearer to him and inclined in; his lips inches from hers permitting her the opportunity to pull away. When she didn't, Nick kissed her delicately on the lips. Cassie got to be strained, breathed in pointedly and filled her nostrils with his aroma.

He waited there sufficiently long to try things out before he felt her resistance dissolve away and she inclined toward his grip. Her lips separated at the vibe of his tongue and her sense elevated. The kiss developed and Cassie was lost altogether

the feelings. She never heard the little crash upstairs u

ntil Ari shouted. That broke the association. Cassie pu

shed Nick aside and kept running up the stairs as quick as her legs could go. She discovered her girl remaining at the end table with an encircled photograph of her father broke on the floor.

"Ari, what's going on with you? she requested grabbing her

little girl and conveying her to the bed. "You could have cut yourself"

Ari was crying. Cassie analyzed her and found no cuts.

"I needed to see my daddy. I'm sad" she said between cries. "I'm sad mom"

Cassie embraced her and began to cry. "No sweetheart, I'm not frantic at you. I'm sad you nearly got hurt".

In the interim Nick had remained in the entryway viewing. He had kept running up the stairs behind Cassie thinking the most noticeably bad. He was soothed the young lady was alright.

"Cassie, I think I ought to go now" he recommended. She didn't disagreee however Cassie felt her spirits dive. She needed to invest this energy with Nick.

"I'll call you today" he said and left. He knew she required time to change in accordance with the circumstances of their fellowship and it would not be simple but rather Nick had trust. He could never surrender trust.

Soon thereafter, Cassie sat tight for Nick to call. She didn't recognize what she was going to say with the exception of that she was confounded as to where they were heading.

She didn't need to hold up long as Nick called just before she went to bed.

"Howdy. I was going to turn in" she said. "I'm sad you needed to clear out. I never got an opportunity to converse with you about us"

Nick breathed in forcefully. "Is there a 'us', Cassie? I have a feeling that I've been tiptoeing around this divider that you have around you and i'm not certain how to get in"

Cassie knew it was valid. How might you be able to simply proceed onward after such a large number of years with the man you knew not your intimate romance?

"I'm sad however I can't simply jump into your arms and let myself go. I don't comprehend what I feel a fraction of the time your around and I don't care for it".

Nick could comprehend that. He knew great that it was so difficult to begin once again once more.

"We'll take it moderate Cassie the length of you will attempt"

Cassie let out a long moan. "I simply don't have a clue. Perhaps I'm simply not prepared yet. I don't know whether I can confer myself to a relationship at this moment and..."

He heard her murmur. Nick needed her to express how

she felt about him yet Cassie wasn't giving anything without end. After the brief close minute they partook in her

house, Nick was slanted to trust she was prepared. He expected to trust that.

"Cassie, There'll be no weight from my end" said Nick. "We should simply begin with a straightforward supper say tomorrow night and we don't need to take it any further if toward the end of it despite everything you feel the same way".

That sounded reasonable to Cassie; supper would be pleasant and she and she wouldn't need to stress. Everything appeared to be so straightforward.

"We can eat. You pick where and I'll be prepared" she let him know. "I just trust we realize what we're doing"

Nick laughed. "You have to unwind and given things a chance to stream. Tail you r heart and possibly it may very well give you the consummation you merit"

Cassie trusted so; Nick Brady was difficult to overlook and working with him may turn out to be a test she would never overcome.

Chapter Eght

Cassie was apprehensive; she exhausted the glass of wine in one swallow. Wearing a dark strapless dress and light blue cardigan, and basic gold studs, she looked shocking. She wore an exquisite gold jewelry given to her by her folks for her birthday years back.

While she made an effort not to lament her choice about today evening time, Cassie couldn't shake the inclination that she was changing their association with this one choice. A thump on the entryway flagged Nick' landing. She got her coordinating grasp and went first floor.

Ni cholas,dressed in a white shirt and dark jeans, his shirt buttons fixed at the top. He held out a solitary tulip when Cassie opened the entryway. She grinned.

"You are so wonderful" he said making her grin even more extensive.

She took the tulip. "Much obliged to you" Their eyes met and held for a brief moment before Cassie turned away "I'm prepared in the event that you are".

"As prepared as we'll ever be". He held out a hand which she took. He drove her to the auto a nd inside minutes they were en route. The drive was peaceful; every lost in their own particular musings. Cassie gradually started to feel casual as the maneuvered into the parking area of a little yet imply Italian eatery.

Situated inside, Cassie was inspired. The stylistic theme was basic yet rich; white cloth secured the tables with delightful silver cutlery and a solitary vase with crisp cut lillies. The room with faintly lit with crystal fixtures hanging over every table nad as the Waitress brought the menus, Nick talked something to her in Italian.

"Another astonishment" said Cassie, "I didn't have any acquaintance with you communicate in Italian. What else is there for me to learn today?

Nick presented his most enchanting grin. "I spent my late spring months amid school voyaging Europe with my siblings. We learnt a tad bit of the dialects here and there and i took up cooking French food once" he answered. "How about we simply say I'm not enthusiastic about cooking"

Cassie snickered. "By one means or another I don't trust you. I saw the way you were in my kitchen preparing treats with Ari. You have a talent for it".

The server came back with the menu and a jug of white wine. In the wake of looking it over, they requested the Linguine in mollusk sauce and the shrimp primavera. They ate peacefully at first and after that Nick made a disclosure about himself.

"I experienced considerable difficulties the right lady for me" he said taking a gander at Cassie. "My family's name is synonymous with riches so I figure ladies were attracted to that more than they were to me as a man. I would never find that right mix in only one lady"

Cassie set her fork down "At the point when was your last relationship?

"Seven months back and before you ask" said Nick, "it finished truly awful. Nadya was infatuated with a companion of mine and I neglected to see it. I thought she was the genuine article yet it turns out she was simply playing along to perceive the amount she could advantage money related from our kinship"

Cassie felt somewhat dismal listening to that. He has never discovered adoration while she had with Joe. How unexpected that now they were attracted together and numerous way they were similar.

"Anyway, I'm certain that is all in the past so we should cheer to the present" Cassie said with much excitement. She was trying to help the temperament. She raised her glass.

"To failing to look back" she said.

"Failing to look back" said Nick.

Supper went easily and Cassie appreciated being there with Nick. The last time she went out for supper was likely a couple of months before Joe passed on. It was at a little eatery around the local area as he had favored not to be far away

from Ari. Cassie recollected that it was French and Joe had whined a ton about the nourishment there. It wasn't an exceptionally lovely ordeal and one that Cassie ought not concentrate on right at this point.

Nick paid the bill and offered Cassie his hand which she acknowledged. It was late and they were both tired; Nick had a bustling day. It was chilliy outside and as they settled in the auto, Cassie attempted to assemble her contemplations. She hadn't needed disagreeable recollections to destroy their night thus far it was a flawless night out. Nick was exceptionally open about his past and that was something Cassie appreciated. He wasn't reluctant to shoulder his spirit to a lady particularly her.

She felt his hand on hers and she turned.

"You're calm. Did you not appreciate the supper? he asked however he was certain she did. Something else was at the forefront of her thoughts.

Cassie constrained a grin. "I was thinking about the past. I figure I lost all sense of direction in time, too bad"

He shook his head. "Try not to be. There will dependably be something that triggers recollections of some other time however as long it doesn't destroy the present then it's no major ordeal"

"It won't destroy it" said Cassie. "We should go to my home and have some espresso. I think that its difficult to relinquish your organization a few seconds ago"

Nick grinned and began the motor. "Home it is then"

A couple of minutes after the fact and they were in Cassie's kitchen tasting on espresso. Cassie felt calm thus did Nick.

He had peeled off his coat and moved up his sleeves; looking exceptionally agreeable at the kitchen counter.

He looked as Cassie tasted some espresso. Nick knew he was going gaga for this lady. She charmed his each idea and he needed her in his life; of that Nick was certain. Cassie would require significantly more before she ever got to that point.

"Let me know about your adolescence" he said. "Did you experience childhood in Lake Charles?

Cassie sat back and looked towards the window to the hack yard.

"My folks were from Jamaica in the Caribbean. I was conceived here and have lived here for all my life" she began. "I never had kin yet my auntie has youngsters my age so I was never truly desolate. Mother and father passed on years prior in a mishap and I was left with no one"

"What happened to your close relative? he inquired.

Cassie swung to face him. "She moved away to Canada with my cousins and we scarcely ever convey"

Nick could comprehend the misfortune. His own particular guardians had kicked the bucket in a plane accident years prior however then they were never near any of their three children. The Brady were a confounded family and Nick learnt at an early age to

fight for himself.

"I let you know I have two siblings, Jonah and Brandon" said Nick. He put his container aside. "We grew up without our folks despite the fact that they didn't passed on until we were grown-ups. We stayed close however I haven't seen Jonah in months. He's the specialist in Spain"

"I have no clue what it resembles to have kin yet I figure cousins can't be that far away"

They talked and talked until Nick saw the time. It was just about two in the morning and neither one of them was drained. They were so charmed in swapping stories, time simply flew by.

Nick stood up and held out a hand to Cassie. She took it and let him pull her up and near him. She could feel his breath all over.

"I need to go. It's 2am and I need to deal with some business in the morning". His hand was on her back making little circle that undermined to break her intention. Cassie attempted to focus.

"I had a flawless time with you Nick. Much obliged to you"

"Do I get a kiss for my exertion? he teased as yet clutching her. Cassie grinned; she appeared to do a ton of that recently because of him.

Without replying, she lifted her face to his and kissed him. It was light and sweet yet Nick needed more. Before Cassie could pull away, he squeezed her into him and took her tongue into his mouth. It was the most choice sensation Cassie had ever experienced. an out of control fire lit up inside her and she let out a moan.

Feeling triumphant, Nick measured her bottom in his grasp and maneuvered her into his crotch. The vibe of his erection against her was the shock Cassie expected to keep her from falling over the edge.

She pushed against him. His mouth lfted a small amount of a second. "Nick I can't...." she started yet he caught her lips once more. This time she pushed harder and he felt the strain in her body.

"Nic, I think we ought to stop while I have the quality to do as such" she let him know. "I can't help myself when you kiss me like that"

He grinned at that idea. "At that point don't overthink this Cassie. Live at the time and let us have our time. I need you and I know you feel the same way".

He held her jaw and lifted her face to him. "Let me know I'm wrong, that you don't feel the same goals that I do".

She couldn't deny it generally as she couldn't deny the air she relaxed. Nick Brady was infectious and Cassie

was getting to be contaminated step by step.

"Will we sit and simply bring a minute to chill off? she asked, frantic for an alleviation.

Nick pulled her back to him. He wasn't surrendering so natural.

"Cassie, quit running from this." he said kissing her nose and after that her cheeks and her neck. Cassie shut her eyes and murmured. It felt brilliant, his lips on her skin and she needed it to continue endlessly.

Nick whispered in her ears. "You ought to never be reluctant to give up and simply live". He kissed her delicately on the lips and as he felt her reaction, Nick started an attack on her deterts that left Cassie gasping hard and needing more

He lifted Cassie in his arms and climbed the stairs to her room. She opened her eyes sufficiently long to enroll where they were and bolted lips with Nick yet again.

He took as much time as necessary stripping her, kissing every last bit of her body along the way. Lifting her yet again, Nick lay her on the quaint little inn himself. Cassie couldn't take her eyes off his body; it was conditioned and manly in each spot. Nick was dazzling.

He returned to the quaint little inn to lie on his back,

pulling Cassie on top of him. She came to in her night

stand and hauled out a condom. Nick held up as she grabbed hold of his masculinity and gradually set up the condom.

Cassie straddled him and filled her body with his masculinity; all of him. The sensation coursing through her was wild, moving her to move quick and hard while Nick clutched her hindquarters. He inclined forward to catch an areola between his teeth, making little nibbles before sucking. Cassie shook increasingly hard until her body blasted into a climax like she had never experienced.

Nick took control and lifted her off him to lay on her back as he entered her yet again. Cassie bolted her legs around his neck and lifted herself to meet his push. Nick felt the beginnings of his peak and dove further into her sex. Cassie clutched his shoulders and kissed him. Nick fell on top of her gasping as Cassie kissed his neck and shoulders.

It felt like perpetually since Cassie had encountered such enthusiastic sex and she grinned as Nick kissed her again and again. They lay that path for a moment before Nick got up and made a beeline for the lavatory. A few moments later, he was back. Cassie snuggled up by him and he held her nearby. Neither one of the ones talked; their bodies had said all there was to say at this moment. They rested for some time before Nick needed to take off.

"I have some business around the local area yet I guarantee to drop by later" he said to Cassie, as yet holding her nearby. "Do you

think it would be alright in the event that I took both you and Ari out to lunch?

Cassie shook her head. "We should simply keep this between us for the present. I would prefer not to confound Ari"

He kissed her brow and separated himself from her.

"We have to discuss this, about us" he started getting dressed.

Cassie sat up and pulled the spreads over her bosom. "There isn't much to discuss Nic, we engaged in sexual relations there's nothing more to it. It doesn't change anything"

He swung to take a gander at her. "Cassie, this wasn't simply sex and I thought you realized that. What I feel for you is more than simply the need to have your body"

"Try not to go there" she got up and recovered her wraparound. "How about we simply live at the time like you said and abandon it at that"

Cassie knew where he was going and possibly he had affections for her that were past physical fascination however she couldn't hear it now. It was far too early for her. Nick

Brady was still her manager.

Nick got done with dressing and took her by her hand. "You and I will talk later. I need to go". He kissed her enthusiastically, dunking his hands into her robe to touch her

bosom. Cassie moaned and inclined nearer just to have him pull away flabbergasting her.

"That is a guarantee of what's to come later". He cleared out her remaining there eyes close and wet between her loin. Cassie reviled deep down and fell once again into her bed. She heard his auto head out. It was scarcely six in the morning and Cassie had a couple of hours before she needed to get Ari at Jessie's home so she did a reversal to rest,

An extremely irritating sound woke Cassie from her fantasy. She turned over and grinned; Nick was doing some exceptionally suggestive things to her. She heard the irritating sound again and this time she opened her eyes.

The doorbell was ringing she understood and took a gander at the clock. It was 11am; way took a break to get Ari.

"Gracious my God, Ari" Cassie had slept late. She rushed down the strides and opened the entryway; changing her robe rapidly.

Jessie ventured inside with Ari and Hannah, She gave the sack to Cassie.

"Look who slept late. More likely than not had a late night" teased Jessie. She knew Cassie was out with a man the previous evening. 'How was supper?

Cassie drove them to the kitchen. She held Ari in her arms. "How was the sleepover sweetheart? she asked her

girl and overlooking Jessie. "Did you have some good times?

"We rested in packs on the floor and ate pizza mama" said Ari. "Close relative jessie says it resembles outdoors yet inside"

Jessie snickered. "It was their thought other than who could oppose these heavenly attendant countenances."

"Ari, take Hannah to the wilderness rec center. We'll be out soon, I guarantee". She looked as both of them limited out the secondary passage.

Cassie began espresso and pulled turkey cuts to make a sandwich. She could enlighten Jessie was anxious to hear concerning her night.

"Have you conversed with your relative of late" Jessie inquired.

"She's home and doing as such well" siad Cassie. "the medical attendant I contracted has made a decent showing with regards to dealing with her"

"Furthermore, Nick?

Vanesaa gazed upward and put on a show to be confounded. She cut the tomatoes to purchase some time.

"Shouldn't something be said about Nick? asked Cassie. "I'm not certain why you're inquiring"

Jessie grinned. "Alright, I'll imagine he's not the man who took you to supper the previous evening"

"Great, how about we imagine. Meanwhile, I need to eat and after that shower" said Cassie, taking a seat at the counter. "I'm eating with him this evening. Will you stay here with Ari?

Jessie gestured. "Beyond any doubt. I should begin charging you for my administrations" She was happy her companion was making the most of her life once more. Cassie should have been upbeat.

They talked while the children played outside. It was past two toward the evening Nick still hadn't called. Jessie went home and Cassie made supper for Ari; her craving was lost. Frustration crawled into her heart as it generally did when somebody didn't keep a guarantee.

She was sleeping six hours after the fact when the telephone rang.

"Hi"

"Cassie, It Nick and before you get all insane on me" he said "I need to apologize I just got back and I know I guaranteed you lunch so what about a late night nibble?

Cassie sat up. She grinned at listening to his voice. "It's past the point of no return for snacks"

"Strawberries and dessert maybe? I'm truly sad about lunch" he said begging her.

"Where are you?

The doorbell rang. Cassie pulled on her robe and went down. She opened the way to discover Nick remaining there with dessert and a dish of strawberries. Cassie roared with laughter and pulled him inside.

"You're crazier than I suspected". She took the foods grown from the ground and strolled to the kitchen. Nick took after behind.

"You look wonderful" he remarked as she spooned frozen yogurt in two bowls and finished it with the strawberries.

She gave him a dish. "I'm wearing PJ's and a shower robe for Pete's purpose" she answered. "Let me know why you didn't appear for our date"

Nick tasted the pastry. "My sibling Jonah appeared unexpectedly and I had some different business I needed to complete today. I could have called however I needed to simply amaze you and drop by"

"Where is your sibling? she inquired.

"Jonah's at my home. He's staying for a couple days before about-facing to Europe. he'd like to meet you"

Cassie verging on stifled on her frozen yogurt. "Why?

Nick answered. "Since he knows you're the one"

This time she definately stifled. It took a while before she

could regain some composure.

Nick was not kidding. "I take it you don't care for being the lady for me"

Cassie pushed the frozen yogurt aside. "Nick, I can't run there with you, not currently"

"At that point when? I'm enamored with you Cassie" he pronounced. "I have been enamored with you for so long at this point"

"That is not reasonable and you know it" Cassie froze. "I don't think right now is an ideal opportunity to examine this. I ought to go. Will you give yourself a chance to out?

Extraordinary. Cassie was really showing him out for pronouncing his adoration to her. Nick pushed the dish aside and tailed her up the stairs.

"What's happening with you? she requested as he close her room entryway. Nick strolled up to her and kissed her which irritated her more.

"I'm not having intercourse with you" she yelled. "Escape my room"

He cleared her up in his arms and dropped her on the bed. "Cassie tune in. You don't need to be terrified and I don't anticipate that you will say you cherish me" he said, then grinned. "in any event not yet In any case, I needed to let you know so you know I'm in this for the whole deal"

Cassie sat up and moved to the furthest side of the bed. "Imagine a scenario where I can't give back the same sentiments. I don't have any acquaintance with you that well and it's just been two or three months since I've covered Joe and I just... I don't know whether I would ever adore again"

She began to wail delicately and proceeded even as Nick drew her into his arms. He saw now why she once in a while demonstrated her actual emotions. She was battling with proceeding onward with her life and being consistent with Joe's recollections. Cassie felt it was imperative to at any rate give herself a year prior to she proceeded onward. Cassie never anticipated that Nick would come into her life a great deal less go gaga for her. The reality of the situation will become obvious eventually in the event that it was all justified, despite all the trouble.

Chapter Nine

Cassie yawned and settled her head further against the pads. She felt her hand brush against something bushy and was startled. At that point Cassie recalled the previous evening.

"Nick" she whispered to herself, He had held her while she cried and after that they both nodded off on her bed. She recollected that him advising her he was infatuated with her and she went ballistic.

Cassie sat up and shook her head. Nick blended yet didn't wake up. She looked over at him, feeling the butterflies once more. Perhaps she required this in her life, a man who was sure and attractive and adored her. Cassie couldn't envision cherishing anybody however Joe yet here she was sleeping with Nick and he was enamored with her.

All of a sudden, she wasn't feeling as terrified as she was the previous evening. The learning that this man cherishes her ought to feel awesome.

She went to the kitchen and made breakfast. Ari would be up any second now and Cassie wasn't certain how to clarify Nick' nearness so from the get-go the morning.

After thirty minutes, she had ham and cheddar omelettes, wheat toast and grapefruit cuts prepared on a plate. In the nick of time Ari descended and overwhelmed her mother's legs in a huge squeeze. Cassie lifted her off the ground.

"Great morning princess" she said kissing her little girl's face. "Is it true that you are ravenous?

"I need treats and drain" said Ari. She squirmed out of her mother's hand and bounced here and there.

"You can have an omelet and a cut of grapefruit" Cassie answered sternly. "Go wash your hands and return". She stuffed a plate to take upstairs while Ari ate in the kitchen. Nick was wakeful.

"Why didn't you descend? she asked putting the plate on the night table. "I put forth breakfast in defense you were ravenous"

"Much appreciated. I thought possibly you would not like to need to disclose to Ari why I was originating from your room"

Cassie grinned and kissed his cheek. "A debt of gratitude is in order for that. I'll be back soon". She cleared out him to have his breakfast and join Ari in the kitchen. Cassie had a great deal to consider and it wasn't only her life that would be influenced, she had Arianna to consider as well.

Soon thereafter with Ari out back playing in her sandpit, Nick and Cassie sat out on the deck. It was cool with almost no wind blowing. You could advise winter was planning to make its introduction. Cassie considered christmas and what her arrangements would be with Ari. She and Joe used to take their little girl on trek to hotter nations; a year ago they went to Negril in Jamaica and it was great.

The white sand shorelines and excellent lodging rooms; tasting rum cream and pina colada on the shoreline while Ari waded in the shallow waters by the sand. It was one of their happiest minute and it was one Cassie could always remember.

Nick went after her hands and held it in his. She took a gander at him and grinned.

"You appeared to be lost in your musings" he watched. He thought about whether she was all the while attempting to acknowledge his nearness in her life. Cassie couldn't get use to the way that he was here with her.

"I was recalling last Christmas. We were in Jamaica for a week" she let him know. "I let you know my folks were conceived there"

"I recall. Do you have arrangements to do a reversal this year?

Cassie shook her head. "I think I'd like to invest it here this energy around. Gwen ought to stay with us, that is whether she hasn't altered her opinion".

That implied Nick couldn't be around, in any event he suspected as much. He was trusting she would incorporate him in her arrangements now that they were as one. Perhaps it would be the ideal chance to visit Brandon and possibly travel a bit. It's been a while since he voyaged.

"I was thinking perhaps we could get together with Jonah for

supper today evening time. He truly needs to meet you and it would get him off my back" said Nick.

Cassie wasn't exactly prepared for that just yet; it would mean she was openly saying they were seeing someone she wasn't prepared for that.

"I can't. I have tons to do before work tomorrow and after that I need to take Ari for a dental arrangement and after that there's the pledge drive for the exhibition one week from now that Carlos has requested that I seat" she answered, "I'm overwhelmed so perhaps next time".

It was a great deal of reasons and Nick knew it. She was holing up behind her work.

"My sibling lives in Spain, Cassie" he said, "there won't be a next time. He leaves toward the end of the week"

"I'm sad Nic, I just can't" Cassie expelled her hand from his and turned away. She concentrated on Ari rather and Nick was irritated. He needed a typical association with Cassie, not something to conceal far from his family and he knew even at work, he would need to imagine she was simply one more worker.

"Is it accurate to say that this is how it's continually going to be Cassie? he asked looking down at the floor. "I can't hold your hand or kiss you in broad daylight or even eat at your table since you're perplexed somebody may realize that we have a relationship?

He at long last gazed upward and swung to her, his eyes loaded with trouble. "Cassie, I adore you. I cherish you and I'm not embarrassed about it. I need to be a piece of your life and Ari's as well however you're so hesitant to discover love and to lose yourself in it. Your better half passed on and I comprehend that, I do however you are still here and you can't overlook what we have between us any more"

Cassie would not like to hear it. She was doing whatever it takes not to cry, not to feel insane for pondering Joe when all she truly needed was to simply to give up and find that affection that she knew was out there, that she knew she could have with Nick.

She stayed noiseless, his words rehashing itself in her mind. Nick was coming clean; Cassie was hesitant to give love access once more. Nick sat tight for her to recognize him however when she didn't he understand that possibly Cassie truly wasn't prepared for this all things considered. He stood and strolled to the secondary passage.

"I need to go. I think you require time and I'm simply pushing you too early" he said. "Try not to stress over Jonah, I'm certain he'll see more than I do. He's not the one in adoration with you"

He cleared out and as Cassie listened she heard his auto head out. She embraced herself tight and did whatever it takes not to consider what he had said but rather it was troublesome when she knew it was valid. Cassie needed to figure out how to give love another possibility.

Part Ten (after four days)

Cassie was occupied in the workplace when Carlos came in. He wasn't more often than not in this early. He looked stressed and that was much more irregular.

"You have been keeping away from me Cassie" he said, sitting on the edge of her work area. "What's more, I think it may have something to do with Brady"

Cassie rearranged paper around her work area trusting he would get the impression she was occupied. It didn't work.

"You should let me know what happened between both of you on the grounds that starting two days back, my executive of aquisitions took a time away"

Cassie gazed upward; she was dazed at the news. Nick hadn't called neither had she seen him in the workplace however Cassie thought he simply required time to chill. She felt an odd feeling in the pit of her stomach; something wasn't right.

"Carlos, I adore you and I believe you're a dynamite manager however whatever you have listened" said Cassie, " my association with Nick is amongst us and it's not up for talk"

Carlos stood and turned towards the entryway. He exited and after that ceased to say to her. "Whatever it is fix it. I need my two best individuals fit as a fiddle for the pledge drive one week from now". He exited her to contemplate her best course of action.

Cassie was going to leave for lunch when one of the assistants dropped by. "Mrs. Smith, there's a man here to see you" he said. "His name is Jon Houston and he said it's imperative"

She didn't perceive the name yet consented to see him at any rate. A tall dim man came into her office strolling with a stick; he clearly had a harm to one side leg. Cassie thought he looked commonplace yet she couldn't exactly put it in her brain.

She stood and offered him a seat.

"I'm sad in the event that I appear to gaze yet I sense that i've seen you before" said Cassie. "Do we know each other?

"I'm perplexed we don't Mrs Smith however I met your better half once" Mr. Houston answered. "What i need to let you know isn't simple for me so I'll simply get to it. I'm certain you have a bustling calendar"

Cassie sat down. "I have a couple of minutes". She grinned yet she was anxious.

The man rearranged in his seat and made a decent attempt not to turn away.

"Mrs. Smith, I was the man your significant other's auto hit out on the expressway. As should be obvious I was harmed and had weeks of restoration. I came here on the grounds that he asked me to"

Joe requesting that you come and see me? Cassie said, abruptly irritated. "Mr Houston, I don't have room schedule-wise for amusements. My better half kicked the bucket in a repulsive mishap and I'm attempting to proceed onward from it. If it's not too much trouble in the event that you'll excuse......"

He held up a hand. "Mrs Winter let me wrap up. He requesting that I let you know that he's sad and he never intended to abandon you. He needed you to realize that he adored you both" he proceeded. "He was biting the dust and he needed to send you a message. I'm simply attempting to submit to his desires. I attempted to at his memorial service"

Cassie recalled now. He was the man under the oak tree. That is the reason he looked so recognizable.

He stood and took his stick close by. "I'm sad for your misfortune Mrs. Smith, I truly am and on the off chance that I could have done anything to help him, I would have. I had a busted leg".

Cassie was close tears by then. She stood and opened the entryway for him.

"Much thanks to you for coming to see me" she said. "I'm sad about your leg. I realize that doesn't help however I'm sad"

Jon Houston exited and left Cassie to manage her feelings.

Back inside her office, Cassie sat gazing out her window w going over the news of his demise in her psyche. Joe had nodded off while driving back to Lake Charles from a business trip. His auto had ran head-on into another and Joe

passed on a couple of minutes after the fact while sitting tight for a rescue vehicle. Cassie had realized that the other driver was truly injured yet she never knew who it was

Cassie was overpowered with blame and bitterness. Joe's message to her was of affection and here she was fleeing from it. All Joe each did was adoration her and made her vibe no not exactly a delightful and immaculate mate for him much like Nick did. All Cassie did was to reject Nick and for what.... to lament over a man who might have cherished her in death and proceed onward with his life.

It never occurred to Cassie that perhaps she felt remorseful in light of the fact that she was at that point in affection with another man. She was enamored with Nick Brady. The disclosure hit her like chilly water in her face. Cassie felt the priGwen tear fall and afterward another and another.

'This can't happen' she said to herself. And after that it hit her. Nick wasn't around. They hadn't talked in four days and she had brushed him off that day on the deck. He adores her and she pushed it aside like it amounted to nothing.

"Goodness God, what was I considering? she asked, "What do I do now?.

Without considering, Cassie got her pack and came up short on the workplace. She took a stab at calling his PDA yet he didn't reply, it went to voice message. She cleared out him a message.

"Nick, I know you have a privilege to be frantic at me and i get it now. I require you, please on the off chance that you get this message.. I require you in my life, Ari needs you as well. If you don't mind give me a chance to back in. I'm sad. I was frightened and ....." she said. "Nick on the off chance that you get this meet me in 60 minutes. I'll be at home"

Cassie called Jessi. "I require you to bring Ari with you tonight. I need to meet somebody later so take her and I'll drop by the house later"

Jessie was concerned. "Is everything OK?

"I'm fine. Simply keep her for me and I'll drop by later. Much obliged Jessie"

Cassie drove home and held up. She sat tight for more than three hours and not a single Nick to be seen. He hadn't called and Cassie knew in her heart that it was past the point of no return. She had pushed him away.

She got her little girl a hour later and made supper. Ari ate while Cassie pushed nourishment around her plate. She couldn't eat and it didn't help that Nick hadn't gave back her call.

By nine o clock, Ari was sleeping and Cassie lay viewing over her. She was such an entirely and tender youngster, her Ari. Joe would have been so pleased with her. Cassie kissed her cheek and pulled the concealment over her. Her mobile phone rang.

"Hi"

"I got your message" said Nick on the flip side. He sounded so inaccessible and cool.

Cassie took a full breath. "I needed to discuss us. I haven't got notification from you in four days Nic. Is it accurate to say that you are alright?

"I'm fine. I took some time off to simply unwind and invest some energy with Jonah before he cleared out for Spain the previous evening" said Nick. At that point after a long delay he asked "Would you say you are alright?

Cassie nearly cried. She thought he was lost to her for good. "I needed to see you and I missed having you around Nic. I understood that I was out of line to you..." she couldn't discover the words to proceed.

"Cassie, I think you and I simply need to venture back and consider what we truly need since it appears we're not in agreement" he answered. "You're not prepared to meet me midway and I comprehend, you require time..."

Cassie shook her head. "No Nic, I comprehend what I need and it's you. I need us and I'm not reluctant to say it. It has taken me this long to acknowledge my misfortune and proceed onward and I know you have been quiet" she said. "I simply need you". Nick said nothing and for some time Cassie thought he may have hung up yet she could hear his tender relaxing.

The sound of the doorbell ringing startled Cassie. "Somebody's at the door" she let him know and ran ground floor. She watched out the window and discovered Nick on her doorstep. Cassie inclined toward the entryway and moaned with help. She opened the entryway and grinned through her tears.

"I'm sad" she whispered surrounding her arms around him. "Nic, I was a blockhead for giving you a chance to walk away...." Before she could complete, he kissed her lips. It was long and profound and everything that he felt for Cassie was laid out in that one kiss. It felt like a lifetime before they separated.

Nick stroked her face delicately. "All I need is for us to have a chance at satisfaction. I need us to appreciate coexistence Cassie. You, me and Ari"

"Also, I realize that now. I ought to have believed my heart yet I let dread aide me and I verging on lost you"

Nick moved her nearer. "I adore you Cassie and I know it alarms you to hear it yet I do love you. Perhaps in time you'll cherish me as well and I'm set up to take that risk in the event that you'll give me access"

Cassie grinned through her tears. She went after him and kissed him, disappointing her gatekeeper and permitting him into her heart. It felt great realizing that Nick was sure about his adoration for her and was willing to give her a possibility. Cassie knew it was more than most ladies would ever seek after.

"I can't envision what I did to merit such love and unwaveringness from you Nick and I guarantee never to baffle you"

He smiled and said. "You never will"

She chuckled and gazed toward him grinning. "Nick Brady, I adore you".

What's more, there it was; the orientation of one's complete self with the expectation that adoration will at last overcome all.

Epilogue

Two Years Later.

On a crisp, summer's night, wearing a white, silk outfit, Cassie warmed up a pot of espresso and poured her a glass. She included sugar and cream as well. She ventured out onto the back yard. She sat down in her rocker as she listened to the music playing nearby. She shut her eyes, laid her head back pondered her time with Nick. Everything made her vibe great. He made her vibe like the main lady on the planet. She knew unmistakably that minutes, regardless of how little, had the ability to change lives. Furthermore, those minutes, similar to a transient star, are gone until the end of time. As she gradually opened her eyes, she deliberately unfurled the letter. She started to peruse in the radiant moonlight:

Dear Sweetheart,
I don't feel that I let you know this almost enough, yet you are truly the best thing that transpired.

There are such a large number of things I adore about you, from your cherishing heart to the way that you cook us delightful dinners.

I generally dream that sometime you and I will move together in the moonlight, as in my fantasies, to our main tune. Until that days comes, I would be content and upbeat if just you would agree to be my significant other. If you don't mind let me know you will.

Yours Always,

Nick

The End.

33904422R00055

Made in the USA
Middletown, DE
01 August 2016